RUMOR GOING 'ROUND

SAMANTHA LIND

SAMANTHALIND.COM

Rumor Going 'Round
Lyrics and Love Series Book 3
Copyright Samantha Lind 2020
All rights reserved.

COVER DESIGN BY *MELISSA GILL DESIGNS*
EDITING BY AMY BRIGGS ~ BRIGGS CONSULTING, LLC
PROOFREADING BY *PROOF BEFORE YOU PUBLISH*

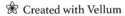 Created with Vellum

CONTENTS

1

TUCKER

"Hey, Tucker, are you going out tonight?" Lee, my best friend and truck mate, asks from his locker located a few from mine. We've both been firefighters since joining the academy right out of high school, both following in our fathers' footsteps.

"Nah, I've got Paisley tonight," I tell him, referring to my four-year-old daughter.

"Oh, I thought you got her tomorrow?" he questions.

"Normally, I would, but Lilly texted me this morning asking if I could pick her up after my shift. She's got something going on and knows that I'll never turn down time with Paisley."

"All right, I guess we'll just have to have a drink in your honor, then." Lee smacks my back as he passes by me, his bag slung over his shoulder as he makes his way to the locker room door.

"You do that," I call after him. "I'll catch up with you next time."

"You're buying the first round, then," he retorts back

as he pushes the door open. Our shift ended about ten minutes ago, and after being on for the last twenty-four hours, I'm ready for a burger and fries with my best girl. Probably following that up with some Disney Junior and then a long-ass shower once she's in bed for the night before I crash myself. It wasn't a super busy shift, we went out on a total of three calls, but they were all spaced out just enough that I didn't get more than a few catnaps during my shift.

"Tucker," I hear my name being called as I walk through the lounge. I look down the hall and see my dad standing just outside his office. I turn his way, coming to a stop next to the sign that reads 'Chief Donald Wild' on it.

"Yeah, Pops?"

"Your mother has been bugging me all day about when she'll get to see Paisley," he tells me, and I can see the way he softens when he says my daughter's name.

"Mom, huh?" I call him on his bullshit. I know Paisley's got him wrapped around his finger and has since the day she was born.

"You know your mother; she can't go more than a few days without seeing her, or she starts having withdrawals."

"I think that *you're* the one that has withdrawals," I tease my dad. "You know either of you can call Lilly and arrange to go pick up Paisley any time you want."

"I know," he admits.

"Well, you're in luck. I'm on my way to go pick her up now. Lilly had something going on tonight, so I'm getting her early."

"I'll text Mom and have her plan on the two of you for dinner, then."

"Sounds good. Tell her I'll be over in thirty," I tell my dad before turning and heading for my truck in the parking lot. I toss my bag in the passenger seat, then slide in. I open the sunroof, letting in the cooler fall air that is finally showing up here in Georgia. Fall has always been my favorite time of year; cooler temps, football, beers by the fire, pumpkins, and Paisley's birthday. I can't believe my girl will be five in just a few weeks. It feels like just last week she was born.

"Paisley Grace!" Lilly calls as I step out of my truck in her driveway. She's rocking her new son on the chair on her front porch. Lilly and I were never together more than a handful of fun nights between the sheets back in the day. We had a few drunken nights, and either a condom was forgotten or broke, but I wouldn't change the outcome at this point in my life. Paisley is the best thing to have ever happened to me. She made me grow up and become the man I am today at the age of twenty-seven. I was a young twenty-two-year-old when she was born. I knew nothing about babies, but I learned fast.

"How's the little guy?" I ask, making polite conversation. Lilly got married to a good guy, Mike, about two years ago. We've all worked together to co-parent the best we can, for Paisley's sake. She didn't ask to be born to parents who weren't together, so no reason her life should suffer because of it.

"He's good. Still working on getting his days and nights straightened out," she tells me as Paisley comes flying out the door, her pink backpack in hand.

"Hey, baby girl," I greet my daughter as she launches herself into my arms. Her little hands wrap around my head, pulling my lips to hers in a smacking kiss.

"I missed you so much, Daddy!" She hugs me tight.

"Missed you, too." I squeeze her tightly, tickling her sides lightly, which has her squirming in my arms. Her legs start kicking, and she almost hits me in the balls, which has me stopping and setting her down quickly.

"Careful there. She'll get you good." Mike chuckles as he stands behind Lilly's chair.

"No, shit." I laugh right along with him.

"Thanks for coming after your shift. She's been pestering me to go see you and your parents. I just couldn't tell her no."

"You know you could have called my mom, and she'd have dropped everything to come and get her," I remind Lilly. Even though Paisley is almost five and I've always been a part of her life, as have my parents, Lilly still has a hard time believing that she can count on all of us to help when she needs it. She didn't have the best home life growing up, so to know she finally found someone with Mike was a good thing, and I'm happy for her.

"I know," she sighs. "I just hate to bug them," she admits.

"It wouldn't be bugging, and you know it. Hell, my dad called me into his office just before I left to ask when I'd be bringing her over. Tried to blame it on Mom wanting to see her, even though we all know he's just as enamored with her as she is."

"Right," she says, chuckling as the baby sleeps on her chest.

4

"Ready to go, Miss P? Nona is expecting us for supper."

"Will Papa be there?" she asks, slipping her hand into mine. I grab her backpack as she waves at Lilly and Mike, then heads for my truck. "Bye, Mommy, love you."

"Love you, too, have fun. I'll see you in three sleeps."

"Of course, he'll be there," I tell Paisley as I help buckle her into her seat.

"Yay!" she cheers, which has me laughing at her antics as I shut her door and open my own.

We live in Monroe, Georgia, a small town just under an hour outside of Atlanta. We're far enough away from the city that the pace of life is slower here, but we still have many people who commute to work every day. Small town life is all I've ever known. I was born and raised in this very town. The type of town that everyone practically knows everyone. I never got away with much as a kid; between the nosy people and my dad being the fire chief, it was hard to get away with anything. But that didn't stop us from being kids and getting into shit.

"How's your baby brother?" I ask Paisley once we're on the road to my parents'. Even with driving across town, it will only take us just under ten minutes to get there.

"He cries all the time," she says, all put out like.

"Babies do that. You used to cry all the time," I tell her.

"Not like he does," she insists.

"I'm sure it can't be that bad," I prod.

"It is, Daddy," she says just as I look up and catch a glimpse of her in my rearview mirror. She's got her hand

5

on her forehead like she's exhausted—the dramatics of a four-year-old. Lord, help me in ten years when she's a teenager.

I can't help but laugh at her dramatics. "Get used to it, kiddo. He's not going to get quiet anytime soon, and he's here to stay."

"I know," she sighs. Maybe she isn't adjusting to having a new sibling very well. I guess some spoiling by my parents is just what she needs to feel better.

We pull into their driveway a minute later, my dad's truck already parked in his spot. "Looks like Papa beat us here," I tell Paisley as I put the truck in park. I hop out, then help her from her seat. She takes off running for the front door, and before she can even reach it, both of my parents are out and waiting on the porch for her.

I lean against the front of my truck, just watching the interaction between the three of them. She's one lucky-ass kid to have my parents as her grandparents. They spoil her so damn much; she's going to be in a world of hurt the first time they learn how to tell her no one of these days. I swear, they've never said it to her once.

"Are you coming in or just standing out here?" Mom calls out to me a few minutes later.

"Just letting the three of you have a moment," I tease her as I join them on the porch. "Smells amazing, Mom; whatcha got cooking?" I ask as the aroma from the house reaches us.

"Meatloaf is in the oven, mashed potatoes and gravy are on the stove."

My stomach picks that moment to rumble, which, in

turn, causes Paisley to laugh at the noise it makes. "Daddy, you's hungry!" she exclaims.

"Sounds like it," I agree with her. I reach out, opening the screen door and holding it for all of us to walk through.

"Wash up now. Supper will be ready in just a few minutes," Mom tells all of us. I follow Paisley into the hall bathroom, where we both wash up.

"We's all clean, Nona," Paisley calls out as we enter the dining room. She heads right for the table, taking a seat in her "special" seat right between my parents.

"Good, I don't let no dirty birds at my table," Mom teases her.

"I's not a bird, Nona," Paisley states matter of factly. Once again, the sass on this one.

"Oh, child." Mom chuckles at her as she sets down a baking dish with the meatloaf. She makes quick work of cutting it into slices then serving all of us one. I pull Paisley's plate over in front of me so that I can cut things up for her. She hasn't quite mastered the use of knives just yet.

"How was your shift?" Mom asks once we're all sitting down.

"Pretty good, just a couple calls," I tell her between bites. My mom is one hell of a cook, and I take advantage anytime the offer is on the table to come over for dinner. When Paisley is with me, I make an effort to eat a well-balanced meal, but when it's just me, I'm a little more lenient on what I make myself, since it's a pain to cook for only one sometimes.

"That's good."

"They were spaced out just enough, though, that I didn't really get a good night's sleep. Just a few catnaps, so I'll be calling it an early night tonight."

"Do you need us to keep her?" Dad pipes in to offer.

"That's okay. I figure after a quick episode on Disney Junior, she'll be ready to hit the hay."

"If anything changes, you know she can stay here with us," Mom reiterates.

"Thanks, I'll keep that in mind," I say to appease them both, but don't have any plans on pawning my daughter off on my parents for the night.

"Paisley." My mom says her name once the table has been cleared.

"Yes, Nona."

"Papa and Nona need some ideas about what you want for your birthday in a few weeks. Do you have any ideas yet?"

"Yes!" she exclaims, bouncing up and down in her seat. "I's wants a puppy, a Disney princess, a bike, and a pink dress," she tells mom matter of factly, like she's been making her list for weeks.

"Wow, you've got quite the list," Mom says as she pulls out a pad of paper to write down what Paisley told her.

"Yep," Paisley agrees with her, and I can't help but laugh at how serious she is about this conversation.

"You ready to go, P?" I ask her once she's done talking to my parents about her upcoming birthday. "Daddy is tired," I tell her, yawning again.

"Sure," she agrees, hopping off the stool she'd sat down on. I watch as she runs off toward the door, stopping to slide her shoes on before she goes to give my parents both a hug and kiss goodbye.

"Thanks again for dinner, Mom," I say as I hug her myself.

"Anytime, honey. Get some sleep, and we'll see you later in the week."

"Sounds like a plan," I tell her as I wave goodbye to my dad.

"So, you want a puppy, huh?" I ask Paisley once we're on the road to my house.

"Yes!" she says excitedly, but then immediately sticks her bottom lip out in a pout that I almost don't see in the quick-second look at her in my rearview mirror.

"What's that look for?"

"Mommy said no puppies," she pouts, adding in some crossed arms as she really sells her disappointment at Lilly telling her no to a dog.

"Maybe not at Mommy's house, but there's always Daddy's house," I tell her, not really thinking about what that is going to mean to her.

"Really?" she questions, her voice picking up in excitement.

"I'm not saying yes for sure, but it's something we can talk about, and I can look into. Getting a puppy is a lot of work, and with Daddy's work schedule, it might not be easy to do. I'd have to see if Nona and Papa would be willing to help with it when I'm at work."

"Nona would help," Paisley insists.

I chuckle at her persistence and faith that my mom will help me out so that she can have a puppy. "Don't go volunteering her for something now. I'd have to talk to her first and make sure that she'd be on board with helping."

"Can I help pick the puppy out?" Paisley asks as if this is a done deal.

"Slow down, P. I didn't say that we were getting a puppy. I just said that it might be an option." I flick my eyes up to the mirror in time to see her little hopes flee her body as the bottom lip comes back out in a pout. "Hey, now, no need to pout. I said we'd talk about it, and I'd look into it. Okay?"

"Okay, Daddy," she agrees with me.

I pull into my driveway and into the garage. Once parked, I help her out of her seat and grab both her bag and my own. "How about a bath or shower, and then we cuddle on the couch for an episode on Disney Junior before bed?"

"Yes! Can I have bubbles?" she asks, skipping into the house.

"Sure." I chuckle at her back as I follow her into the house. I drop our bags off in our respective rooms before heading to the bathroom next to her room. She's already dumping the bucket of toys into the tub before I can even get the water turned on. I get it all set up for her, bubbles included. While she plays in the water, I set out her vitamins and get her toothbrush ready for after she's in PJs.

"I loves you, Daddy," Paisley tells me once we're cuddled up together on the couch about a half-hour later.

"I love you, too." I kiss the top of her head as we watch some princess show she wanted to watch. I feel myself nodding off by the time the episode ends. "Ready for bed?" I ask, picking her sleepy body up from the couch.

"Yes," she says, yawning into my neck. I carry her to her bed, tucking her in for the night. I kiss her forehead before turning on the small night light on the nightstand.

"Sleep tight," I tell her in a whisper before I leave the room, shutting the door behind me. I check the doors to make sure everything is locked up tight and then head for my shower and then into bed.

2

LINDSAY

"ARE YOU READY YET?" MY BEST FRIEND, ALLISON, ASKS AS I finish applying my mascara. We've been friends since forever, basically since we were in diapers. Our moms have always been BFF's, so it was inevitable that we'd be the same way with all the time we were together; it also helps that we're only a few weeks apart in age.

"Yep," I call out as I clean up my mess in the bathroom.

"It's just Joe's; you don't have to look perfect," she replies, referring to the local bar we're headed out to tonight. We're meeting a few other friends there for a drink or two. It's ladies' night, and it has been one hell of a week at work. I've been a nurse in the ER going on six years now. I was hired almost immediately upon returning home from college and haven't looked back since. I love it in the ER. There is never a dull day. We've always got patients to keep us busy; you never know what may come through the door. From patients with the stomach flu or a broken bone to major accident victims, we don't see much downtime.

"All right, let's go," I say, grabbing my debit card and driver's license from my big wallet and sliding them into a small little wristlet, along with some cash and my Chapstick.

"I can't wait to get out on the dance floor and shake our asses off tonight," Allison says on the way to the bar. It's not far from my little two-bedroom house.

"I know. I need to release some steam, and a drink or two and some time on the dance floor sounds like the perfect way to unwind," I agree with her.

"And not having to work tomorrow is the perfect excuse to let loose tonight," she adds as I pull into the parking lot. Ladies' night is sometimes more popular of a night than Friday and Saturday nights can be, and by the looks of how full the parking lot is already, tonight is going to be that way. "The one thing better that I can think of to let off some steam would be some good dick, but I don't think that's on either of our horizons tonight."

"God, what I wouldn't do with some good dick," I agree with her. It's been a while, okay, more like six months, since I've slept with anyone and the last person was my asshole ex, who really wasn't the best when it came to sex. He was all about getting his own but not great with making sure I got mine all the time.

"I mean, I'm sure you could easily find a man or two that'd gladly take you home for a fun night between the sheets," Allison says, bouncing her eyebrows up and down as she laughs.

"Not that desperate," I tell her, "yet," I add for good measure.

"Girl, you need to live a little. A good one-night stand might do you good. There's just something about some no strings attached sex that will set you up for a few weeks."

"Yeah, I'm still just fine for now. I've got a few different BOBs to keep me company on lonely nights," I tell her, referring to my drawer of vibrators that have gotten their share of workouts over the past few months.

"Girl, tell me about it. Sometimes you've got to do what you've got to do."

We make it inside the bar, looking around for the group of friends we're supposed to meet here tonight. I see a few of them already at a table. Since we live in a small town, it isn't like I don't know just about everyone here, and just like high school, everyone is grouped off. Allison and I stop off at the bar; Joe's working tonight.

"What can I get you ladies tonight?" he asks, wiping the bar top in front of us off before placing down two cocktail napkins.

"I'll take whatever light beer you've got on tap," Allison tells him.

"I'll have a raspberry mojito, please."

"Coming right up," he says, reaching for a glass to put under the beer tap to fill Allison's order. I watch him mix up my drink next, already salivating over how good his mojitos are. "You ladies want a tab tonight?" he asks, setting my glass down in front of me.

"Yep," Allison says. "And we'll be over there." She points at the table that already has six or so people around it. It's hard to tell from this angle if they're all at one table or if some of them are part of the next table and just chatting with our group.

We reach the table and find our friends Becky, her husband Todd, Rob, David, and his girlfriend, Trisha. At the table next to them are some other guys, Tucker and Lee, who were a year ahead of Allison and me in school, along with a couple other guys I don't know, but recognize as firefighters that work with Tucker and Lee. Working in the ER, we see the paramedics and firefighters regularly.

"You made it!" Becky calls out, hopping off the barstool she was perched on to give me a hug.

"Of course!" I call out over the music already playing. "Wouldn't miss ladies' night for anything." I set my drink down on the table and say my hello's around the group. Allison moseys her way over to Lee and Tucker's table. She's been flirting with Lee for months. The two of them just need to get it over with and hit the sheets. I'm actually surprised that they haven't already, especially with how pro one-night stands she is.

"Are you ready to shake your asses?" Allison asks Becky and me a few minutes later when the opening chords of "Champagne Night" by Lady A comes on.

"Let's go!" Becky yells as she tugs on our arms. I laugh at my friends' excitement and follow both out onto the dance floor. We sing along to the songs as we shake our asses and sway to the music. This was precisely what I needed after three long days in the ER.

The DJ changes things up and slows things down. Before I can escape the dance floor, I feel a set of hands slide along my hips, sending tingles straight to my core. "Dance with me?" A voice I'd know in my sleep fills my ears. *Tucker.*

I turn in his arms, sliding my own around his neck as I rest my head on his chest and we start to sway around the floor to the song. I don't even really hear the sound of the music with my ear pressed against his chest; all I hear is the pounding of his heart.

"How have you been?" he asks after a minute or so of swaying.

"Good, just busy with work and everything," I tell him, looking up at him and into his chocolate brown eyes. "How's Paisley?" I inquire about his daughter. She's so damn cute.

"A spitfire, like always. Hounding me like crazy to get her a puppy for her birthday next week."

"Every girl needs a puppy," I tell him, trying to help his daughter out.

"Not you, too," he groans. His hands shift slightly, one practically covering my entire lower back as he holds me close.

Much like my relationship with Allison, I've known Tucker for practically my entire life. He's a year older than me, but in a small town, you play with everyone around you. We hung out with the same group of people, for the most part, so we have always been friendly. If I'm honest, I've always crushed on him but never got the same vibes in return. I've never been the outgoing and bold type that would ask a guy out, so those feelings and the attraction won't go anywhere unless it comes from him.

"How's work? I haven't seen you in the ER lately."

"Same shit, different day." He chuckles. "Now that we're back to full staff on the paramedic side, they don't need our help as much with riding along in their rig."

"That makes sense," I say, shifting my hands after I realize I'm playing with the longer strands of his hair at the base of his neck. "Paisley will be, what, five next week?" I ask, turning the conversation back to his daughter.

"Five going on fifteen, but in about two weeks," he grumbles, but I can feel the love that he has for her in that grumble. "She's going to either give me gray hair or make me go bald before she's ten," he muses.

"I'm sure she isn't that bad." I laugh at his demeanor.

"She isn't. Just the level of sass that comes out of her is amazing. I have to remind myself that she's only four. Lilly and Mike having a baby a few weeks back has been a big adjustment for her. I think she's taken it a lot harder than anyone expected her to. Most kids are super excited for a new sibling, but she's been the complete opposite."

"That has to be a hard adjustment," I sympathize with her. "She's so used to being the center of everyone's attention, and now she's playing second fiddle to a new baby."

"Yeah, she begs to come to my house when I'm not working. Tonight was the first night that she didn't ask to come over before our normal time," he tells me.

"Ah, well, at least she knows that she's got a safe place with you that she can get away from being around him, when needed."

"Yeah, I'm just trying to make sure I don't enable the behavior. We don't need her learning at five how to

17

manipulate Lilly and me when she's not getting her way at one of our houses. That's one of the reasons I'm struggling with getting her the dog or not. Lilly already told her no at their house right now. I know that deciding to get one for my house is a little different than, say, buying her a car down the road, because the dog wouldn't just be hers, but mine, as well. But I also don't want to do anything that would make Lilly's life more stressful because it's affecting Paisley's attitude when she's with her and not with me."

"Can I just tell you how amazing it is to hear of two parents that actually work together for the better of their kid rather than constantly backstabbing one another. I hear all about it at work, and I always just feel sorry for the kids caught in the middle."

"We've always done our best since she was born. She didn't ask to be born to two parents that weren't together and never would be."

"Y'all are seriously the best," I tell him as I squeeze his biceps before stepping back from his embrace. The song we were dancing to has long since ended, but we just stood there talking. "She's lucky to have the two of you as parents."

Tucker follows me back to the two tables that our friends are corralled around. I notice some questioning eyes from a few of the guys, probably wondering what is up between us, but try not to read into it much. I sneak a glance at Tucker, and it doesn't appear he notices the looks we're getting, so I go back to my friends, who have also come back to the table for a drink.

The evening passes by, filled with so much laughter

and dancing, and was just what I needed to let loose and enjoy myself. I don't get out nearly enough, so I'm glad that Allison convinced me to come tonight.

"I'm ready to call it a night; how about you?" I ask Allison a little before midnight.

"I think I'm going to go home with Lee. Are you good to get yourself home?" she asks, chewing on her bottom lip as she hangs onto Lee's side. His arm is around her waist, possessively. It appears that they're finally going to give in to whatever push and pull has been going on between them for a long time.

"I'm good, be safe, and call me if you need anything."

"I'm good," she assures me. "Text me to let me know when you make it home."

"Yes, Mom." I roll my eyes at her, laughing as I do.

"Don't give me no sass, young lady," she retorts back. "Are you good to drive?" she asks, all joking aside.

"I can give you a ride if you need one," Tucker slides into our conversation. "I only had one beer, and that was hours ago."

"I'm good. I only had two drinks all night and a few glasses of water. I can get myself home, but thanks for the offer." I smile up at him.

"Okay." He smiles down at me.

"Be safe, y'all. And don't do anything stupid," I remind Allison and Lee.

"Yeah, wrap that shit up," Tucker tells his best friend, slapping him on the back as Lee and Allison head for the door. "I can't believe he finally convinced her to go home with him," Tucker says, shaking his head in disbelief.

"About damn time. They've been skirting around it for a long-ass time."

"Yeah, they have," he says, running a hand through his hair. I watch as his fingers slide through his locks and have never wanted to feel a man's hair in my fingers like I do at this moment.

I pull my keys out of my front pocket, patting my back one to make sure my wristlet is still there. Feeling it, I drain the remainder of my water and am ready to head home. "You leaving?" Tucker asks.

"Yeah," I say as I yawn, covering my mouth with my hand. "I need to get home and to bed. It's been a long week, but I have the next few days off and I'm looking forward to relaxing. First thing on my agenda tomorrow is sleeping in. No alarms, no appointment, or commitments; it will be glorious," I tell him.

"Let me walk you out; I was ready to go myself."

"Thanks," I tell him, just as his hand lands on my lower back. The feeling of his hand against me, even if we do have the layer of material between us, is like a brand on my skin. I don't think he can tell the effect he has on my body, or at least I hope he can't right now. My body is humming just from his simple touch. I'd probably be crazy enough to tell him yes if he asked me back to his house tonight.

We make it out into the parking lot, and it has cleared out a lot since I arrived with Allison earlier. As we approach my car, I hit the button on my remote and unlock all the doors. Tucker takes a few large steps to get in front of me, reaching my car before I do. He opens my door, holding it for me as I pass by him. "Drive safe," he says gruffly once I'm seated and have secured my seat belt.

"Always," I tell him, flashing him a sweet smile.

"Give me a minute to jump into my car, and I'll follow you home to make sure you make it okay," he says, catching me off guard a little.

"I'll be fine, Tucker. It's only a few blocks away."

"And I have to go right past your place to get to mine, so I'll follow you anyway; just give me a second to get behind you," he insists. I just roll my eyes at him but can tell that he'd be pissed if I didn't wait for him.

"Fine," I huff in mock annoyance, "but I promise I'll be just fine, Tucker." He grumbles some more as he shuts my door, then takes off in a jog across the parking lot to his truck. I watch as his lights flash, then the interior light comes on when he opens the door. He fires it up just as soon as he slides in, and pulls out of his spot, coming across the lot until he's near me. I pull out of my own spot and into the road. Just as I said I would, I make it the few blocks to my house and pull into the driveway. I tap my brakes a few times, letting him know that I'm all good, and he flashes his brights at me as he continues on down the road.

One of the perks and drawbacks of small-town living is that everyone is in each other's business and ensures everyone is safe. While I appreciate what he did, it was also wholly unnecessary, but alas, it's over, and I'm home.

3

TUCKER

I MAKE IT HOME AFTER FOLLOWING LINDSAY FROM THE BAR. Having her in my arms tonight was a double-edged sword. On one side, it was the best feeling. Her curves are what wet dreams are made of. On the other, it was a painful night of having to continually adjust my dick as discreetly as possible. Each time I'd watch her shake her ass out on the dance floor, my cock would swell in my jeans. The few moments I held her against my body, I don't know how she missed it. She was flush against me the entire song and then some.

I grab a beer from the fridge, popping the top before I chug half of it down as I lean against the wall. The night out was just what I needed to blow off some steam and hang out with the guys. I take my beer and head for my bathroom for a hot shower before crawling into bed. Unlike Lindsay, I have commitments tomorrow. I'm supposed to pick Paisley up mid-morning, and before I do that, I wanted to go grab some groceries, as my fridge and pantry are looking pretty bare at the moment.

I step under the hot spray of water, setting my beer on the ledge. Nothing better than beer to enjoy while the water works my tight muscles. I grab my body wash, squirting a fair amount into the palm of my hand, then working it over my chest. My hand slides down my abs and around my hard cock. I can still feel Lindsay as if she was pressed against me here in the shower. The smell of her shampoo or perfume still fills my nostrils, and I can't help but stroke my shaft at the memory of her tonight. I brace one hand on the wall and give in to my primal desires, thinking of no one but the sexy woman who has filled my dreams since I was a teenager waking up to wet dreams.

My head falls forward as my eyes close. I let my imagination take over, picturing what she looks like naked. I've seen her a handful of times in a bikini, so I've got some ideas on what she'd look like out of it. I think of her perfect tits and how I want to get my mouth on them, teasing her hardened nipples until she's arching beneath me, begging for more. I'd slide down her body, dropping kisses along her skin as I make my way to her pussy. I stroke my cock a little faster at the thought. Just the idea of tasting her, making her come on my tongue, has my balls tingling and ready to blow my load. I slow my strokes, squeezing my shaft to prolong my release.

My mind wanders back to being between Lindsay's legs. My tongue on her clit as my fingers slide in and out of her tight channel. My fist tightens and speeds up as I stroke my cock, no longer holding back on my orgasm. "Fuuuuck!" I yell as my orgasm barrels out of me, my cum coating the wall of my shower. I lean into the hand braced against the wall as I enjoy the endorphins rushing through my body after that powerful release.

Once I've regained my head, I spray off the wall, not wanting to leave a mess to clean up later—that's never a pleasant time.

Once out of the shower, I towel off, wrap it around my waist, and stand at the sink to brush my teeth and trim my beard down. I can't let it get too long, as it can interfere with how tightly my mask fits at work. Once done at the sink, I grab my dirty clothes, fishing my cell out of my jeans pocket before dropping the clothes in the basket. I snag a clean pair of boxers from my drawer and step into them on my way to my beside.

I pull back the blanket and top sheet, then drop on the bed, sliding between the cold sheets. They feel good against my hot skin. I place my phone on the cradle, making sure that it's charging before I roll over and let sleep claim me for the night.

Tuck: Hey, man, you up?

Lee: Yeah, but I just got out of bed. Had a good night, if you know what I mean.

Tuck: I'm sure you did. I was with you when you left the bar last night. I know who you took with you.

Lee: The night did not disappoint.

Tuck: At least one of us got some action last night

Lee: If you'd grow a pair, you could have gotten laid last night

Tuck: Whatever, man, enough about the lack of pussy in my life at the moment. I woke up with an idea this morning.

Lee: And what was that?

Tuck: The big football game is next weekend, we're both off that day, so why don't we pull together a big party. We can have a bonfire afterward out back.

Lee: I'm game.

Tuck: Figured you would be. We can start spreading the word, tell everyone to BYOB and a dish to share. I'll fire up the grill, and I'm sure I can convince my mom to make up a few sides.

Lee: I'm sure Mama Wild will be all over that.

Tuck: You know it.

Tuck: What you got going on today? Allison still at your place?

Lee: She left about ten minutes ago. I don't have anything going on; when are you picking P up?

I LOOK AT THE TIME, AND I'VE GOT ABOUT TWO HOURS until I'm supposed to be over at Lilly's to pick her up.

Tuck: A couple of hours. I need to go grab some groceries first. Want to come over later? We can grill up some steaks or something.

Lee: Sure, I'll head that way at some point. Let you have some father-daughter time before I crash and take over as P's favorite person.

He loves giving me shit that my daughter loves him the most. He can keep dreaming on that one. No one will ever knock me out of that spot. Not my dad, and definitely not my best friend. Whoever my daughter grows up to fall in love with better be one hell of a man if he wants the spot. I won't hand it over quickly.

Tuck: See you later fucker.

I drop my phone on the bed next to me and force myself to get up and moving. I need to get some shit done before going to the store and to pick up Paisley.

Once dressed in a pair of jeans and a T-shirt, I make my way out to the living room, where I flip on the TV before making my way into my kitchen. The open floor plan of my house allows me to see everything. I cook up an easy breakfast of eggs, bacon, and toast.

Once fed, I start my list of things to get done around here. I try my best to keep a clean house; that way, nothing takes me long when it is time to clean. I scrub down the counters before running the steam mop over all the hardwood floors in the house, consisting of the kitchen, living room, hall to the front door, and the hall down towards the bedrooms. With things clean, I head for the grocery store.

I'm walking down the aisles, going through the mental checklist of what I need for the next few days, knowing what Paisley prefers to eat and making sure I've got everything she'll want. We're pretty lucky that she isn't a super picky eater. She easily eats all her fruits and veggies, which not many four-year-olds do.

"Hey, Tuck." I hear the sweetest voice call my name from a few feet away. I look up from the stand of apples I'm in front of and see Lindsay standing, filling her own bag of apples.

"Mornin' Linds," I greet her, a smile tugging at the corner of my lips. She's an angel on legs and just about takes my breath away in her leggings and flannel shirt. "Did you get to sleep in like you'd hoped to?" I ask, remembering what she told me just last night.

"I did!" she confirms. "It was glorious. I can't remember the last time I slept in so late."

"That's good; glad your plans worked out."

"No Paisley this morning?" she asks.

"I'm headed to get her when I leave here," I tell her.

"Do you have any fun plans?" she inquires.

"Not really, just hang out. Lee is coming over later."

"I'm sure that will turn into trouble." She smirks.

"He can be just that. Have you talked to Allison this morning?" I question.

"No! I sent her a text but haven't heard anything. Have you talked to Lee?"

"I was texting with him earlier. Sounds like they had a fun night. She was at least there until after nine," I tell her.

"That little hussy," she mutters, and I cannot help but laugh.

"Hey, I'm putting together a football party slash fall bonfire party next Saturday. Would you be interested in coming? Allison is welcome to come with you. Lee will be there." I toss out the invitation. "Just a casual, fun event. BYOB and a dish to share kind of thing, plus, I'll have the grill going."

"Maybe; I'm not sure what's going on next weekend just yet. I might have to cover a shift for someone, but if I don't, then it sounds fun."

"Would love to see you there."

"I'll text you later in the week. Does that work?" she asks as she places her fruit in her cart.

"Perfect," I tell her.

"Good seeing you this morning, have a good time with Paisley," she says before pushing her cart down the row. I watch as she goes, her ass wrapped tight in her leggings is causing my dick to spring to life in my shorts.

I grab a few more kinds of fruit and make my way to the checkout. Seventy-five bucks later, and I'm headed out to my truck. With my groceries loaded, I hop in the driver's seat and head to pick up my girl.

"DADDY," PAISLEY SINGSONGS MY NAME FROM THE BACK seat.

"What's up, buttercup?" I ask as I turn the radio down so that I can hear her better.

"Can you get me a puppy for my birthday?" she asks, and I groan a little inside. What did I get myself into?

"I don't know, baby. I need to think about it some more," I tell her honestly.

"Pllllllllllllease????" she asks, dragging out the word.

"You drive a hard bargain, you know that?"

"Daddy, I's wants a puppy, though," she reiterates.

"I know you do, and I said I'll think about it."

"But my birthday is soon, so you have to think fast," she tells me, that sass coming out again.

"You've got me there," I tell her, laughing at how she just called me out.

"I still need to talk to Nona and Papa to see if—and I mean *if*–I get you a dog, that they'll be able to help with it when I'm at work. Someone would have to be able to let it go outside and feed it when I'm working, and you're at your mom's," I explain to Paisley.

"Nona will help me," she says matter-of-factly.

"You sound pretty confident about that." I laugh.

"She always tells me she'd do anything I need," she states.

"I guess she does, doesn't she?" I give my daughter that one. Mom does always tell her that she'll always be there to help her with anything she needs. And to an almost five-year-old, apparently, that translates into taking care of her dog when she's at her mom's house, and Dad is on shift.

We make it back to my house; I carry the groceries into the house, following Paisley in. She beelines it for her room, dropping her backpack off that she likes to bring between our homes. While we both keep all the necessities like toothbrushes and toothpaste, a hairbrush, and her hair products along with clothes, she has a special lovie that she's slept with since she was a baby, along with whatever toys are her favorite that day.

I make quick work of getting all the food put away before I get the steaks for tonight marinating so they'll be ready whenever Lee shows up, and we're ready to grill.

"Paisley," I call down the hall, "are you ready for some lunch?"

"Yes, Daddy," she answers as she comes out. Once she reaches the kitchen, she climbs up on one of the bar stools at the counter.

"What would you like today?" I ask as I lean on the counter facing her. I can't believe just how big she's gotten lately. She's turned from a toddler into a big girl practically in the blink of an eye, and I don't know if I'm okay with it. I can't believe that at this time next year, she'll be in kindergarten.

I watch as she makes a funny scrunched up face, obviously thinking hard about what she wants. "PB and J," she finally states.

"Now, that, I can do," I tell her, pulling the bread out of the cabinet along with the peanut butter. "Strawberry or grape?" I ask, walking over to the fridge to grab the jelly.

"Strawberry!" she exclaims, wiggling on the stool.

I grab the jelly and make my way back to the counter. I pull out enough bread to make three sandwiches, one for her and two for me.

"Alexa, play country music," I call out, and music turns on from my smart speaker. We love listening to music while Paisley watches me cook. We'll often stop to have dance parties when a good song comes on. I start to shake my butt as I spread the peanut butter when a Luke Bryan song comes on, and Paisley falls into a fit of giggles as she watches me. "What's so funny, baby girl?" I ask as I push a plate across the counter to her. I placed the sandwich, along with half of a banana, on her plate and a glass of milk in front of her. I've got this dad shit down to a science some days.

"You's funny." She giggles some more. I don't stop shaking my butt until Luke's song comes to an end.

"Just trying to keep a smile on your face," I tell her as I take the stool next to her. We both dig in to the best damn PB and Js out there.

We finish up our lunches, then head outside to play. I've got a decent amount of land, with my own pond and trails that we take the quad out on, which Paisley loves doing.

4

LINDSAY

"YOU'VE GOT SOME DISHING TO DO." I SMIRK AT MY BEST friend as she walks through my door. All I got was a text saying she was coming over *and* bringing wine.

"Food and wine, and then I'll dish," Allison says, taking the bags she's carrying straight to my kitchen. She sets everything down and starts pulling things out. I help her get things assembled; she's got all the fixings for a charcuterie board. I pull my board out, and I start assembling the meat, cheese, and crackers on it while Allison pulls my wine opener out and cracks the bottle open, pouring both of us a healthy glass.

"Okay, so," she finally breaks her silence as we make our way into the living room. I carry the board, and she carries our glasses and two plates. I set the board down on my coffee table and take one of the plates and glasses from her hands. "It was a crazy night. I lost count of how many times we did it," she finally tells me, her cheeks pinking up just a bit.

"So, it was good, then?" I ask, smirking at her.

"Um, yeah. That boy, I mean, *man* knows how to work it. He was, ahem, *very talented,* to say the least."

"Good for you. Way to work it." Knowing they've been circling each other for *years,* I suspected things were going to be explosive when they finally got together. "So, was it a one-night kind of hook-up, or are y'all going to do it again?" I ask, pun totally intended.

"We didn't define anything, just left it kind of open-ended," she tells me, shrugging her shoulders slightly. We both fill our plates and sit back on the couch, turned so we're facing one another. I pull my legs up so I'm cross-legged, and Allison sits with hers tucked to the side.

"Did you get *any* sleep?" I prod before taking a sip of my wine.

"Nope," she says, popping the p. "Well, not until I went home. I shit you not, we probably had sex ten times, and he fucking came every time and made me come. As I said, that man is fucking talented in the bedroom."

"Sounds like a fun night." I bounce my eyebrows at her. "Glad it was mutually satisfying."

"I'll be thinking about it for a long time, that's for sure. I also don't know how I'm walking today," she says, laughing.

I sigh, thinking about what it would be like to be sore because a man fucked me all night. My mind immediately roams to Tucker. The T-shirt that he had on this morning hid absolutely nothing of the muscles that make up his arms and torso. The way his abs rippled under his shirt had my mouth watering as I stood across from him, placing apples haphazardly in my bag. Those damn muscles are the reason I ended up with enough apples to last me a few weeks. I might just have to make a pie or something with some of them so they don't go bad before I can eat all of them.

"Oh, before I forget, I ran into Tucker at the grocery store today, and he invited both of us to a football and bonfire party next Saturday. I told him that I wasn't sure if I could make it since I told Betty I'd cover her shift if she needed me to."

"Sounds like fun," she says.

"Tucker said Lee will be there," I add.

"I figured that." She laughs. "Those boys don't do much without one another. Kinda like us," she quips.

"Yep," I agree with her before we fall into a fit of giggles. I love our comfortable, carefree nights that we have like this. Nothing pressing. Just good food, good wine, and most of all, my best friend to talk about anything and everything that life throws at us. We've been having nights like this since we were kids. Obviously, our drinks of choice have changed over the years, as have our topics of discussion, but at the end of the day, I know that I'll always have this girl in my life, just as she knows I'll always be right here in her corner cheering her on.

Lindsay: Hey Tuck, just wanted to let you know that I can make it tomorrow night if the invite is still open! I don't have to cover the shift tomorrow night, after all.

I SHOOT OFF THE TEXT QUICKLY, WANTING TO MAKE SURE that things are still going for tomorrow night. I haven't heard from him since I ran into him at the store last Saturday, and Allison hasn't talked to Lee, either, so we're both in the dark about tomorrow night.

"I texted Tucker about tomorrow," I tell Allison as I plop down on a chair across from her in the cafeteria at the hospital. We're both on our lunch break. Thankfully, the ER is on the slow side today, so we actually get a break today to scarf down some food.

"Oh good, what are you thinking of bringing?" she asks as she crunches on some carrots and ranch.

"I was going to bake an apple pie with all those damn apples, and maybe a pan of those bacon-wrapped smokies that everyone goes crazy over."

"Yes, I love those stupid things." She approves my ideas. "I figured I'd make up a batch of cookies or brownies. Can't go wrong with chocolate."

"I like the way you think," I tell her as I bite into my sandwich. "Are you nervous to see Lee again?" I ask between bites.

"No, but I am interested to see what he's like tomorrow. Part of me thinks that he's going to be all up in my business, but part of me thinks that he got what he wanted, and now he's moved on to another conquest."

"What do you want it to be?" I question. I already know that, deep down, she'd like for there to be something more with him. She's only crushed on him since we were in high school.

Allison shrugs her shoulders, giving me a look. One that says so many things, yet nothing at all. "I just hope he doesn't act like nothing happened, but I also don't want the cold shoulder. You know how easy it is to get hurt, and I'm not looking for that to happen," she admits.

"If he hurts you, I'll knee him in the balls," I tell her.

Allison laughs, and my job here is done. "I fucking love you," she tells me as she wipes off the table in front of her with her napkin now that she's finished her lunch. "I always know you've got my back."

"Damn straight. But I also know it goes both ways."

"Absolutely," she says, just as both of our phones start buzzing. We carry special phones that each nurse is issued. We both look down at our screens and see the page that we've got multiple MVA patients on their way in to us.

"Looks like it is go time," I say as I toss my trash, and we both take off for the ER.

"We've got a husband and wife on their way in; information from the EMTs is that a car turned right in front of them," Betty tells us as we reach the nurses' station. Allison and I both pull-on protective gowns and gloves, along with face shields, just as we hear the sirens pull in. I meet the ambulance in the first bay, along with Dr. Knight.

"Female, fifty-five, pain in the left foot and abdomen. No loss of consciousness, all vitals have been stable," the EMT tells us as we make our way into the treatment area.

"Transfer on my count, one, two, three," Dr. Knight calls out as we all lift the sheet that is under the patient.

"Ma'am, can you tell me your name?" I ask the patient as I check the IV the EMTs placed in her arm.

"Julie, Julie Smith. Is my husband okay?" she asks, trying to move her head to look for him.

"I'm not sure, ma'am," I tell her. "I'll see what I can find out for you, but for now, are you in any pain?"

"My foot and belly hurt," she says. Her foot appears to be fractured, and the belly pain could be from the seat-belt locking on impact.

"Mrs. Smith," Dr. Knight addresses her. "Does it hurt when I press here?" he asks, palpating her abdomen. We get the answer when she wails in pain. "I'm sorry, ma'am," he apologizes. "Administer two milligrams morphine, IV push. We're going to need ultrasound down here ASAP after x-ray," he tells me, and I do just as he asks.

I work fast to get Mrs. Smith's pain under control. When the x-ray tech shows up a few moments later, we all step back while they take the images that Dr. Knight has ordered. I take a moment to step over a few treatment bays to see if I can get any information on Mr. Smith. I catch Allison's attention, and she nods her head quickly. That is my one clue that while he might be in bad shape, it doesn't appear to be life-threatening.

I head back to Mrs. Smith, stepping back up next to her now that the x-rays are all done. "I poked my head over to check on your husband, and they're working on getting him fully checked over. I promise I'll keep you updated once they've had the chance to fully evaluate him," I tell her as the ultrasound tech shows up with her mobile machine.

"Thank you, dear," she says, squeezing my hand.

"This will be a little cold," the ultrasound tech warns

before she squirts some gel on Mrs. Smith's abdomen. She starts to scan her, and I sigh in relief when no internal bleeding is found. Her pain is just from the trauma of the seatbelt locking upon impact. While that will cause some nasty bruising, it will be a lot easier to heal from than an emergency surgery to fix internal bleeding would be.

"Good news, Mrs. Smith," Dr. Knight says. "You won't be needing surgery today. We'll get your foot booted and keep you for some observation for a few more hours, but otherwise, I think that you'll heal just fine. You'll need to follow up with an orthopedist in two to three days for the foot."

"Thank you so much, doctor. How's my husband?" she questions, still holding on to my hand.

"He's still being assessed by one of my colleagues, but I do believe he's possibly going to need surgery. I do know they asked for a consult with the general surgeon on call. Lindsay, here, can check in with his team and get some more information for you," he tells her, nodding his head in my direction.

"Let me go check on him now," I tell her, squeezing her hand before I pull my own from her grip. I press the button on her bed to help her sit up some before I leave the bay to go check on her husband.

"Can I get an update for the patient's wife, who is in bay one?" I ask Dr. Murray.

"We're prepping him for surgery. He's got a bleed in the intestines and possibly his bladder; we'll know for sure once we get him open. Other than that, he's got a few abrasions from the glass. He should be good to go in a few hours. I anticipate him needing one, maybe two nights inpatient, depending on how his pain management is post-surgery, as long as we don't find anything we're not expecting," Dr. Murray tells me.

"Thank you, I'll update his wife," I tell her as I step away and back to my patient. I quickly update her. "Before he's taken to surgery, I'll try to get you over to him. How's the pain?" I question.

"It's getting much better," she tells me, and I can tell that the pain meds have finally kicked in.

"I'm going to go grab you a wheelchair, then we can take you over to see Mr. Smith."

"Thank you, dear," she says, and I head for a chair.

5

TUCKER

"LET'S GET THIS PARTY STARTED!" LEE CALLS OUT AS HE unloads the back of his truck. I walk over, giving him a hand. I grab two cases of beer along with a bag of ice.

"How much did you buy?" I ask, looking at how much more he's got back here.

"Didn't want to run out before the night is over." He smirks. "It isn't a party if we run out of beer."

"Yeah, but everyone coming is supposed to bring their own, remember?" I ask as we walk around to the back deck, where I've already got a few coolers ready to be filled with ice and beers.

"What time are people showing up?" he asks, popping the top on a beer before sucking half of it down in one gulp.

"Anytime they want, but I figure most won't show up until closer to kickoff," I tell him, looking at my watch and seeing that we still have around an hour until then. "Let's get everything else unloaded and set up, and then we can kick back," I suggest and take off for his truck again.

Another trip to Lee's truck, and we've got everything out. I set up a folding table on the deck to hold food and drinks that others bring. We get the condiments pulled out, as well as the buns for the burgers and hot dogs that I'll throw on the grill once more people show up, and everyone is ready to start eating. My mom dropped by earlier with large bowls of her homemade baked beans and coleslaw. That woman is a saint, and I'll love her until the day I die.

"I'm surprised Paisley isn't here tonight," Lee comments as we kick back on the couch. The pre-game coverage already started. Bulldog games are big here, but make it against a rival like Alabama, and people go crazy.

"I figured tonight wasn't the best night for her to be around. I didn't want it to get too rowdy, so she's having a night with Nona and Papa since she'd normally be here with me. She was a-okay with that plan, so were my parents. They're probably spoiling the fuck out of her right now," I tell him, taking a drink of my own beer.

"That girl is going to walk all over all of you when she's a teenager," he muses. He might be joking and trying to bust my balls about it, but I'm scared shitless that he's not kidding.

Our attention is pulled to the sound of car doors closing and voices hollering outside as people start to arrive. I open the screen door, seeing that some of the guys from the station have arrived, along with their significant others, if they have them.

I welcome everyone in, showing them where best to stash drinks and food. Everyone knows each other, so I don't have to worry about introductions as more and more people arrive as we near kickoff. I keep my eye out, hoping like crazy that Lindsay will show up sooner rather than later. I've had this deep desire to see her again. My hands itch to have her in my arms, so if she shows up tonight, I'm going to have to make that happen. Hopefully, she'll stick around for after the game when we light the bonfire and start the music. I could go for dancing with her in the dark, holding her body close to mine as we sway together.

"Yo, earth to Tucker," Lee says, smacking the back of my head as he flashes his other hand in front of my face.

"Fuck off," I clap back at him, laughing at the sting of pain from him hitting the back of my head. "What the fuck do you need?" I ask.

"You've got company," he tells me, pointing out the back door and onto the deck. Standing there next to the cooler is a vision. Lindsay is talking with some of the other women in attendance, a beer in her hand, so she's obviously been here for at least a couple minutes. I can see her in profile, and she's never looked more beautiful. Her hair is down in loose waves, jeans encase her slender legs, and the Bulldogs shirt she's got on proudly displays her alma mater, that she's rooting for tonight. *My kinda girl!*

"Well, fuck me," I muse under my breath, but loud enough, apparently, that Lee hears me.

"You'd better make a move on that if you don't want someone else swooping in and locking it down," he tells me, smacking a hand against my shoulder, this time leaving it resting against me as he squeezes it and points out to a few guys who appear to be circling the group of women outside.

"Fuck," I curse as I head that way. No way in hell am I going to stand by while one of these fuckers tries to swoop in and steal the one woman I might actually want to pursue for more than a quick lay.

"Ladies," I greet the group of women talking. "Can I get anyone anything or show you where anything is?" I offer the group.

"We're good," they all chime in at the same time. I look around the circle, my eyes lingering on Lindsay for a few moments longer than they do on anyone else.

"Glad that you could make it; I've saved a seat for you inside if you wanted to come watch the game," I offer. I hadn't really, but she can take my seat. I'll fucking stand, or better yet, she can sit on my lap while we watch the game.

"Thanks," she says, leaning in slightly as I pull her into my side for a makeshift side hug. *What the fuck am I doing? A fucking side hug. Facepalm.*

I lead her into the house that is now filled with at least thirty people all milling around chatting as they watch the game. My hand finds the small of Lindsay's back as I lead her over to where I'd been sitting, and, thankfully, the spot is still empty. She looks around and realizes that it's the only open spot front and center. "I can't take your spot, Tuck," she says, shortening my name, and all I can think of is her saying that while I fuck her. My dick springs to life in my jeans.

"Sit down, fucker! Didn't your mama ever tell you that

43

you're a better door than a window?" Lee calls out from where he's standing behind the furniture.

I just flip him the bird as I plop down on the chair, pulling Lindsay with me and into my lap. "If you don't want to take my seat, then you can just sit with me," I whisper into her ear as I push her hair off her shoulder and out of the way. My lips ghost along the skin of her neck, and I watch as it puckers from the sensation. Her entire body shivers in my arms, and I know that my breath on her skin has affected her, hopefully in a good way. "Cold?" I ask, just as the majority of everyone bursts out in a loud cheer. I look at the TV to see a replay of the quarterback throwing the perfect spiral pass to one of the receivers, who runs the ball in for a touchdown, putting the Bulldogs up six to nothing to open the first quarter of scoring.

"No," she says, squirming slightly in my arms, and it's at that moment that I realize the problem with her sitting on my lap like this. Her perfect little ass is going to be rubbing against my dick all night long, giving me the largest set of blue balls known to man. I adjust her slightly; hopefully, my dick isn't pressing too much into her backside and giving me away right now. I find it hard to concentrate on the game with Lindsay in my lap, but the game eventually pulls me in for a little bit.

Halftime rolls around, and the Bulldogs are leading twenty-one to fourteen. "I should go fire up the grill. You want anything other than a burger or hot dog?" I ask Lindsay before I stand her up so I can get myself up and to the grill.

"No, either sounds perfect," she says, turning to give

me a sweet smile. I squeeze her hip with one hand and tuck a lock of hair behind her ear with the other before I break away from her and head for the grill.

"Food time!" I call out to everyone as I fire it up. It doesn't take me long to have a line of people waiting as they all load up plates with food. Not that everyone hasn't been snacking on the other food that everyone brought, but now that its halftime and the grill is going, people are hungry.

It takes me all of halftime and part of the third quarter to get everything grilled and my own plate assembled. I grab a couple beers from one of the coolers and make my way back inside. I find Lindsay back in the recliner we'd both occupied earlier, fully engrossed in the game. Bama has managed to tie things up, making this an exciting game, for sure.

I set the beers down on the end table next to the chair and stand not entirely behind the chair, but not exactly beside it, either, kind of between the two. I make sure I'm not blocking anyone else that's behind the couches standing to watch the game. I scarf down my burger and fixings. Mom's baked beans are just as amazing as they always are.

"You should have told me you were back. I would have let you have your seat back," Lindsay says when she notices me standing back here.

"I'm good; I didn't want to spill on you," I tell her as I finish off my plate. "But, I did bring you a beer if you want it." I offer her one of the bottles.

"Thanks," she says, accepting the bottle after I pop the top off. I watch as she brings it to her mouth, her lips wrapping around the top of it as she tips it back. *Fucking hell, when did watching a woman drink a beer cause me to turn into a fucking flagpole?* I adjust myself as discreetly as possible as she swallows down the cold liquid.

"Would you like to sit down now?" she asks, patting the open cushion that she's not covering.

"Only if you don't go anywhere," I tell her, going big or going home. I want this woman like I want my next breath. I think it's about time I stop beating around the bush, man up, and make a fucking move.

"Okay," she agrees, and stands as I round the chair. I sit back down, and she follows me back until we're in the same position we were for the first half of the game.

"Are you sticking around for the bonfire?" I ask once the game ends. Georgia pulled out the win with a touchdown as the clock expired in the fourth quarter.

"Do you want me to?" she asks, her head still resting on my shoulder, where it's been for the last few minutes.

"Wouldn't have asked if I didn't want you to," I tell her. "Whatever happened to Allison coming tonight? I haven't seen her around."

"She's not much for football, but I think she was planning on stopping by for the bonfire. I'm supposed to text her when it gets going," she says, sitting up so she can grab her cell off the end table. It was poking the two of us earlier because she had it tucked in her back pocket, she'd set it there, so it was out of the way. I watch as she unlocks the screen and pulls up her text messages. I look away, not wanting to invade her privacy as she taps away at the screen. "She'll be here in ten," she says, standing and sliding the phone into her back pocket.

"I'm sure Lee will be happy about that," I muse.

"You think so?" she asks.

"If the little bit that I actually heard out of him about last weekend has anything to say about their time together, it was something he's definitely looking to repeat."

"I just hope he doesn't break her heart," she tells me honestly. "She's not as flippant about things as she likes people to think."

"Give him a chance. He just needs the right woman to lock him down."

"And you?" she asks.

"I just need a chance," I tell her. The idea saying all I need is *her* is on the tip of my tongue. But I can't spring that on her right now. We've only ever been friends. Whatever this is that is sparking between the two of us is something that I'm definitely going to attempt to unpack and see what comes of it.

"You coming?" Lee shouts at me from the back doorway.

"Hold your horses; we're coming," Lindsay calls out to him, laughing as she takes in his impatient look.

I slip my hand into hers, linking our fingers together. I bring our clasped hands up to my mouth and kiss the back of her hand. "Come on, we'd better get out there before he lights my entire backyard on fire."

Lindsay laughs as I tug her toward the back door, and it's one of the best sounds I've heard in a long-ass time. *Since when does a woman's laugh rank up there as one of the best sounds I've ever heard?* "Isn't he a firefighter? Isn't that the exact opposite of what y'all are trained to do?" she asks, still laughing.

"You'd think." I laugh right along with her. "But give that man some lighter fluid, and he goes a little crazy."

"Well, then go save your property," she encourages once we're out on the deck. I leave her side, taking off in a jog to catch up to Lee. We safely get the bonfire pile lit, the flames lighting up the night sky.

Everyone that is still here starts making their way over to the fire. I head back for the porch, turning on the outdoor sound system with some country music. I also flip on the outdoor lights, lighting up the pond's pathway and the deck with twinkly lights.

With all the food put away and the table out of the way, the deck opens up and becomes a makeshift dance floor. A few couples make their way over when an older Tim McGraw song comes on. I look around to see if I can find Lindsay. My hands itch to touch her again, to hold her close like I did during the game.

I finally find her on the other side of the fire, sitting on one of the logs that surround the fire pit, talking with Lee and Allison, who obviously showed up while I was busy getting things going. I take in the way Lee is sitting behind Allison so that her back is to his front. His hands rest on her thighs as they face Lindsay. I sneak up behind her, mirroring the way Lee is sitting as I sit behind Lindsay. I slip a hand around her torso, my thumb finding a sliver of exposed skin where her shirt has ridden up from the top of her jeans. I draw lazy circles with the pad of my thumb, taking advantage of any inch of her creamy skin I can get my hands on.

48

We sit around the fire, shooting the shit with our friends for what feels like hours. The four of us trade stories from some of the calls and patients we've all dealt with over the years in our respective jobs. With Allison and Lindsay both nurses, and Lee and I both firefighters, we've all got some crazy times beneath our belts.

"I should probably head home," Lindsay finally says as she yawns. Her head has been resting back on my shoulder for the last thirty or so minutes, and I can feel her getting more and more tired as she melts into me as the minutes pass by.

"I've got a spare room if you want to crash here for the night," I offer.

"That's okay. I'm not far. I'll be okay to make it home," she says, yawning again.

"You sure? I don't mind at all."

"I'll be fine, Tuck," she says quietly, pressing a little more of her weight into me.

"Then let me walk you to your car. You're okay to drive, right?" I ask. I know she hasn't had any alcohol since we've been sitting around the fire.

"I'm as sober as can be," she assures me as we stand up. Lee and Allison are both getting ready to leave, as well, and seeing as how we're the last four out here, I guess it's time to call it a night myself.

"What's your schedule this week?" I ask as we make our way out to the driveway.

"I work Monday, Tuesday, and Wednesday day shift," she tells me.

"Are you always on days?" I ask.

"Yep. Not many nurses rotate. Unless you're a float

nurse or covering for someone else, you work the same shift; the only thing that changes is what days we work. It doesn't always work out, but I'm usually three on three off, but sometimes I'll work three on two off or three on four off. Just kind of depends on people's vacation schedules and if we've got anyone out for maternity or some other kind of extended leave."

"How many days are you off after your three on this week?" I ask, mentally rolling through my own work scheduled to see if we've got any aligning days off.

"Three," she says as we make it to her car.

"Did you have anything inside that you brought and need?" I ask, realizing she doesn't have much with her.

"Nope. The dishes I brought were in tossable containers."

"What did you bring?" I ask, realizing that I don't even know if I had whatever it was.

"Apple pie and those little bacon wrapped smokies with brown sugar on top."

"Damn. I think both were gone before I got to the food. Damn operating the grill."

"Sorry. Maybe if you're nice, I'll bring you a pie to have all to yourself."

"Don't tease me, woman. You might have just unlocked the way to my heart." I wink at her, the light from the front porch bright enough to light up the driveway so that we can see one another.

"Good night, Tucker, thanks for inviting me. I had a great time," Lindsay says before she moves to open her car door. I step aside, grabbing it for her and holding it open while she slides in behind the wheel. *I should have fucking kissed her when I had the chance,* rolls through my mind as I watch as she drops her keys into the cup holder, and presses the start button.

"Night, Linds, text me and let me know that you made it home okay, please," I ask, adding the please onto the end.

"I'm a big girl, Tuck," she says, rolling her eyes at me, but I know she's not mad about my request, if the smile on her face tells me anything. "But, I'll appease you and send you a text when I make it home."

"Thanks, I'll sleep better knowing that you made it home in one piece."

"Night," she says, reaching for her door. I push it closed for her, then step back from the car so that she can pull out. I stand and watch until I can no longer see her taillights in the dark. I turn around, realizing that, at some point, Lee and Allison left, as well.

I know that I've got about ten minutes until Lindsay makes it home, so I head to the backyard, pulling the hose with me to spray on the coals that are still going. With those properly extinguished, I pick up as much as I can see and fit in my hands on my way back to the deck. I'll get the rest tomorrow when I can clean up in the daylight.

After locking up, I make my way into my room. I'm just pulling my shirt off when my phone buzzes in my pocket. I slide it out and see a message from Lindsay.

Lindsay: Made it home in one piece. {winky face}
Thanks again for the amazing night.

Tucker: Anytime. I'm glad you had a good time. Sleep tight.

Lindsay: Night.

I set my phone in the charging cradle on my end table so it can charge for the night. I head for the bathroom, and ten minutes later, after a quick shower, I'm sliding between the sheets with only one woman on my mind. *Lindsay.*

6

LINDSAY

"So, what's going on with you and Tucker?" Allison asks as we walk around the lake. The fall weather hasn't really shown up yet here in Georgia, even if we are inching closer and closer to Halloween.

"I don't know," I groan, looking up to the sky, hoping for some answers myself. "I don't know what to make of him, if I'm being honest. It all started that night we went to Joe's for ladies' night. He came over and danced with me, and it was just different. He held me like I was his, if that makes sense?" I say, almost as a question.

"Oh yeah, he had all kinds of *mine* vibes going on that night," she confirms.

"After you left with Lee, he walked me out to my car and then followed me home to make sure I made it okay. Then the football game and bonfire the other night. You should have seen him during the game. I still can't get over the feeling of him holding me for almost the entire game. At first, he just tried to play it off as there not being enough seats, and there weren't, so I'll give him that. But,

53

Allison, he was so damn sweet and attentive to me. And you saw him when we were out around the fire."

"I did, and I'd say that man has it bad for you. About time he realized it," she says, bumping her shoulder against my own as we continue walking. "Have you heard anything from him since?"

"Nope, but I think he's working, or maybe he's got Paisley and is busy, or maybe I'm just reading into things too much," I ramble.

"Definitely not reading into things. That man wants you and bad. Mark my words."

"Maybe."

"But the bigger question is, do you want him?"

"He makes me feel..." I pause, thinking about just what I feel when I'm around Tucker. "He makes me feel alive, like I'm beautiful and important. Even in a room full of people, he made me feel like I was the most important person there. It was almost like he was in tune with me and knew what I wanted or needed before I could even voice it. Like he was connected to my soul somehow. Thinking back on it, you could almost find it creepy how in sync we were without even trying."

"That's almost some soul mate-level kind of stuff going on," Allison points out.

"I guess only time will tell if anything happens between us."

"Maybe you should call him or shoot him a text?"

"I don't know. Maybe."

"We've got the next three days off, maybe he'll have time off, and y'all could go out on a date? Or better yet, invite him over and cook for him. Wear something sexy, have some music going... Tempt that man right out of his clothes and into a heap of orgasms," she muses as we approach the parking lot where my car is. "I bet that man knows how to work the pole, if you know what I mean." She winks at me as she bursts out, laughing at her pun.

"You're incorrigible." I laugh right along with her.

My conversation earlier with Allison has played on repeat all day. Should I just bite the bullet and text him? Have I just been trying to see more than was really there the last few times we've hung out?

I turn my attention back to the movie I turned on earlier, *Forever My Girl*. I fell in love with this story from the book and was ecstatic when it was made into a movie. With my focus on the TV, I stop stressing over the whole Tucker thing, at least for a little bit.

Once the movie ends, I grab my cell and realize I missed a text from my cousin Reese, earlier. Rather than texting her back, I just tap her name and call her. I've missed her so damn much, but she's out there kicking ass as one of the biggest names in Country music. Between her moving full-time to Indianapolis, where her husband plays professional hockey, and her tour schedules, I hardly ever see her anymore.

"Hey!" Reese's sweet voice fills my ear as she answers her phone.

"Hey, yourself. How's life?"

"It's great!" she says, laughing. "Stop it," I hear her say, almost as if the phone has been pulled away from her face. "Sorry about that; Austin was pestering me."

"No problem, how's married life treating you?"

"It's really great, well, at least it is when your spouse isn't pestering you," she says, punctuating those last few words as if she's trying to get her point across to her husband. I can't help but laugh right along with her.

"Let me talk to my cousin for a few minutes, and then I promise to give her back to you," I call out, hoping that Austin can hear me.

"I put you on speaker, so he heard all of that," she says before I vaguely hear him grumble something in the background. "Okay, he just left the room for a few minutes, so you've got my full attention, so tell me everything!"

"Not a ton to tell. I work, come home, sleep, wash, rinse, repeat," I tell her. "You're the one with the interesting and ever-changing life. How's Nicole doing?"

"She's doing great, getting so big. I really need to find some time to make it home. How's Nana?"

"Feisty as always."

"I'm sure she is. Maybe we can come home for Thanksgiving. Austin will have to leave early, if he can come at all. They've got a road trip right after the holiday. I think they leave on Friday for, like, four nights, but Nicole and I could come for ten days or so, will you be around?"

"Don't have anywhere else to go, and if you're coming home, you damn well know that I'll be here. I could even take a few days off to spend with y'all. Lord knows I've got the time off saved up, and need a good reason to use it."

"You know you could always come out here for a few days if you want to get away," she offers. "We have more than enough room in this big house, and I'd love to have you here. I could take you to one of Austin's games, maybe introduce you to one of the single guys," she muses.

"A game sounds fun, but I'm not so sure about one of the guys, even if they do look pretty hot in all that gear."

"Girlll…" she says, drawing out the word. "I don't know how I'm not already pregnant again. I swear, my husband comes home, and I just want to jump him."

"You go, girl. If I had a husband as hot as yours, and that was as sweet as him, I'd probably be jumping him every chance I got."

"God, we're bad." She laughs.

"That we are," I agree with Reese.

"So, any prospects on the horizon?" she questions.

"Has Allison been texting you?" I ask her, almost wondering if my best friend has been conspiring with my cousin.

"Nope, why? Does that mean that there is someone?" Reese perks up.

"Maybe," I tell her, sucking in a breath, not really knowing where to start. "You remember Tucker?" I ask, sucking my bottom lip in and biting it.

"Tucker Wild?" she asks.

"The one and only," I confirm.

"Yeah, what about him? Wait, didn't you crush on him *hard* all throughout high school?"

"I wouldn't say *all* of high school, but some of it."

"Anyway, go on about Tucker," she instructs.

"We've had a few encounters? Moments? I don't know how the hell to describe them," I tell her honestly, and then go on to lay out the details of each of our last few encounters. She listens intently as I tell her everything.

"Okay, so that's a lot to unpack, but I agree that it sounds like something is brewing. What's your gut telling you?" she asks.

"To let it unfold and see what happens. I know some of that is I want that perfect romantic experience. The movie-worthy swoony moment of being swept off my feet, falling in love with my soulmate kind of love. I want what you and Austin have."

"And you deserve every one of those moments, and if Tucker is your soul mate, then I have faith that he'll deliver all of them."

"How can you be so sure?" I ask.

"Love is..." she trails off for a moment. "Love is a funny thing. It will leave you hurting and confused one moment and so over the moon the next that you'll feel like you're floating and won't come down to earth again. It's definitely a rollercoaster on the emotions. Austin and I had a lot of obstacles in our way when we first met, the distance being the biggest. We were forced to become friends and get to know one another long before we were ever able to connect on any other levels, thanks to my tour schedule back then. I know you don't have any obstacles like that in your way, and you and Tucker already know one another, probably pretty well since we all grew up together. But I'm sure that there are still lots for the two of you to learn about one another. Hell, I'm still learning things about Austin, and we've been married for a few years and have a kid."

"Thanks for the advice. I think I'm going to just let things develop if they're going to develop, and if they don't, then it wasn't meant to be."

"Maybe give him a nudge or two?" she suggests.

"I'm not sure I'm that outgoing," I tell her. "What if I've just read everything wrong and he doesn't have those kinds of feelings toward me. Then I've gone and made a fool of myself."

"Lindsay, if that man held you in his lap for an entire football game, he's got feelings for you, or at least one hell of an attraction going on."

"We'll see," I say. "Okay, now tell me, when am I going to get new music from you? Have you been working on anything new?"

"I have! I'm actually dropping a surprise single in just a few weeks! I'll send you a copy of it to listen to. It's so fun, and I can't wait for it to hit the radio. I think this next album is going to be my best yet! I've had so much fun helping with the writing of these songs the last few months and can't wait to channel that energy into the studio and then out on the road with a tour."

"Will you do another full tour?" I ask. I know since Nicole was born that she's only done some shorter jaunts, playing maybe ten shows over a month or six weeks rather than a show every night or two, going city to city for months at a time.

"Possibly. I know my record label wants me to, but that's a lot of logistics to take a baby on tour, and a husband on the road with a completely different schedule. Makes for lots of feathers in the air, but I'll probably have one, and we'll just have to hire a nanny to travel with me. I can't expect any of the grandparents to go on the road for months at a time, and Austin can only commit to the off-season dates, so it's something that we'll have to get used to at some point, at least until he's ready to retire, but that's a long way down the road, Lord willing."

"If I didn't love my job so much, I'd say you could take me with you, but I don't know how well that'd work out long-term."

"I'd so take you up on that offer, but I understand."

By the time we're ready to hang up, hours have passed, and it was just what I needed to feel ready to tackle life, and whatever is going on between Tucker and me.

"I'll shoot you that song and let you know ASAP if we'll be heading that way for Thanksgiving."

"Sounds good. Give my love to Nicole and Austin," I tell Reese before we disconnect.

I plug my phone in on the end table by the couch and make my way into the kitchen, looking for something to eat for dinner. I don't find anything appealing, so I grab my keys and phone and head out to my car. I don't really know what I want but find myself pulling into a local BBQ place in town. I head inside, and place and pay for an order to-go, then take a seat on one of the benches in the waiting area. They usually don't take long to box up to-go orders, so I just scroll through my Instagram feed while I wait.

"I'm here to pick up the order for House 57," I hear a

male's voice say. I look up and see someone dressed in a Station 57 dark blue T-shirt and uniform pants. Upon closer inspection, I see that it's Lee. Once the hostess turns to go check on his order, he turns my way, seeing me sitting here.

"Hey," he greets me, closing the space between the two of us.

"Hey, Lee," I greet him. "How's it going?" I ask.

"Good," he says, a cocky grin tugging at his lips. "How are you?"

"I'm good, just grabbing some dinner and then heading back home. How's your shift?"

"Good, been pretty laid back so far. Hopefully, the rest of the night will be the same way," he says just as the hostess comes back out with multiple bags in her hands.

"Lindsay, I've got your order here, and Lee, I've got part of yours; it will just be another minute or so on the rest," she says to both of us.

"No problem, I'll just run this out to the truck and be back to get the rest," he tells her, flashing her a quick wink.

"Tucker's out in the rig," he says as he backs against the door, pushing it open as he does, and allows me to step through it. I see the fire truck parked along the far side of the parking lot, a few guys all loaded inside of it. They have to travel together just in case they get called out when away from the firehouse.

"I see that," I tell him watching Tucker as he jumps down from the fire truck. He's dressed in the same uniform as Lee, the firehouse T-shirt pulling tight across his sinewy muscles. Even from across the parking lot, I can tell that it's tight. I see the moment that he realizes that I'm next to Lee, as his face lights up in the sexiest smile that has my knees going week and a jolt of need that makes me want to rub my thighs together to relieve it.

"Hey, Linds. What are you doing here?" Tucker asks as he closes the distance between the truck and where Lee and I have made it to in the parking lot.

"Just picking up some dinner. Didn't have anything that sounded appealing at home, so take out it is for me tonight," I ramble.

"Same for us. No one wanted to cook, so BBQ it is. How was your week at work?" he asks as Lee continues on to the truck, handing the bags of food over before he turns to head back inside for the rest of their order.

"It was good, kind of a quiet week."

"That's good. Hey, you up to having dinner together tonight? You can meet us over at the firehouse, and we can take ours out to the picnic table out back."

"Um," I stall, biting my bottom lip as I think over his invite.

"Come on, give me a little break from these guys," he says, practically begging, and doing his best to give me the saddest puppy dog eyes I've ever seen a grown man use.

"Okay." I crack up, laughing at his antics. "But only if you promise to never do that again," I say, circling my finger around whatever it is that his face has contorted into.

"Yes!" He pumps his fist into the air like he's just won

a prize. "And no more of that," he assures me, a smirk back on his face.

"Why don't I believe you one bit?" I ask, rolling my eyes at him.

"Scouts honor," he says, holding up three fingers next to his shoulder.

"Let's go, Wild!" one of the guys calls out from the truck. When I look over, I realize that Lee is already back in the truck, and all the guys are staring our way. "Food's getting cold," the guy, who I don't recognize, calls out.

"I'm coming!" he yells back at them. "Just follow us to the station; you can pull around back to the parking lot, and I'll meet you back there in just a couple minutes," he says before heading back to the truck. I get in my own car and follow them out of the parking lot and the few blocks to the station. I do as he instructed, finding a parking spot near where a few tables are set up outside, along with a grill and some outdoor games for the guys to play when they're here, but waiting to be dispatched out.

"You were off today, right?" Tucker asks once we've both dug in to our food.

"Yep, had a lazy day, mostly. Allison and I went on a walk around the lake this afternoon, but other than that, I was just at home. I did get to talk to my cousin, Reese, for a little while this afternoon!"

"How's she doing?"

"Good, really good. I miss her so damn much, but she's going to try and come home for Thanksgiving in a few weeks."

"Still crazy to think that she's accomplished everything that she has," he muses.

"I'm so damn proud of everything she's accomplished."

"And from what I can tell, she hasn't allowed the fame and fortune to go to her head."

"Oh, God, no. She's still the best, down to earth person you'll ever meet. Her husband, too. They're perfect for one another."

"Good for Reese; she deserves it," he says as he finishes off his container of food. I don't know how in the hell he packed away all of it, as the portions they serve are huge. I always end up with a couple meals out of just one order.

"What are your plans for the rest of the night?" he asks as I close up my box.

"More of what I did this morning, movies and sleep. I already cleaned my house, so I don't have that to keep me busy, then early to bed, as I'm covering a shift tomorrow. What time are you off?" I ask just as the alarms go off. Tucker jumps up from the bench.

"Sorry, gotta go!" he calls out as he takes off running for the front of the firehouse. "I'll talk to you later!" he calls out over his shoulder just before he heads into the bay where the trucks are parked. I clean up our trash and take my leftovers with me. I wait in my car for all the emergency vehicles to pull out before I leave the parking lot. They turned left while I turn right and head home.

7

TUCKER

I ROLL OUT OF MY BED AT THE FIREHOUSE, MY BACK POPPING as I stretch my tired body. Our call last night was a long call. A fire broke out on a farm, first in the fields, and then reaching one of the smaller equipment barns. Thankfully, no one was hurt, but with the gas and other chemicals that were in the barn, things got a little hairy when they caught fire and sent a ball of flames in the air. We worked with another firehouse for a few hours to get everything out.

The new shift of guys will be here in about thirty minutes, and I want to be ready to head out as soon as they're here. My bed at home is calling my name, and then I need to pick up my girl.

"Mornin'," my dad calls out as I make my way to the coffee pot.

"Morning," I grunt more than say. I need coffee before I'm going to function today, apparently.

"You guys did good work last night," my dad compliments as he stands sipping his own coffee.

"Yeah, it was a late night, but no one was hurt, so I'll call it a win."

"The report I got from Chief Bower said that everyone worked efficiently and that the landowner was thankful that we kept the fire from reaching their other barns or, worse, the house."

"They were very concerned about that, but it would have taken a lot for the fire to eat up that much distance," I tell him as I finish my first cup of coffee, filling my cup right back up for my second cup this morning. "Unfortunately, the one barn was a total loss, along with all the equipment inside of it. A few tractors and I'm sure a lot of tools."

"All stuff that can be replaced," Dad states. Being in this business as long as he has, he's the first to remind everyone that stuff is replaceable, people and pets aren't. So, if we can respond to a call and leave with everyone intact, we've accomplished the most important part of the job, according to him. "Are you bringing my grand-daughter over for dinner tonight?" he asks, changing the subject to his favorite one, Paisley.

"Maybe, let me see what transpires today. I'm going to head home here in a little bit and crash for a few hours. I need to catch up on some sleep before I do anything."

"Okay, well, just let Mom or I know so we can plan for dinner."

"Will do; see ya later, Pops," I tell him, smacking him on the shoulder. He heads down the hall toward the offices while I head to the locker room so I can grab my things from mine and head out. A few of the guys from the next shift have started to trickle in, so I visit with them until everyone is accounted for, and my shift is officially released for forty-eight hours, when we're expected to report back for our next shift.

———

I WAKE UP A FEW HOURS LATER, FEELING LIKE A WELL-rested man. I head first for the bathroom, where I step into the shower, turning the water up as hot as I can stand it and then letting it beat on my body. The tension melts from my tired muscles as the water works its magic. While I'm showering, an idea springs into my mind, so I set about to make it happen.

I'm out of the shower, dried off, and dressed, all within fifteen minutes. I run a comb through my wet hair, attempting to style it before I head out.

I pull into the parking lot at the hospital a few minutes later. I only know that Lindsay is here because she told me that she was covering a shift today right before I ran out on the call last night. I assume it will be in the ER, since that's where she usually works.

I walk through the automatic doors, walking into a waiting room that only has a few people in it. The aide at the desk looks up, smiling when she sees me. "Tucker, what brings you in today?" she asks.

"I was actually hoping to talk to Lindsay, if she isn't busy?" I ask, realizing that my plan might not work.

"I think she's available, just have a seat and let me check," Mary says before she disappears into the back. I do as she says and find a seat facing the doors that lead back into the treatment area of the ER. A minute or so later, the doors open, and Mary is standing there, waving for me to join her. "She's at the nurses' station, you know the way, correct?" she asks as I pass by her.

"Yep, I've got it from here," I assure her. I walk the short distance to the nurses' station, a few of them all sitting around chatting amongst themselves.

"What do we owe the pleasure of you visiting us today?" asks Debbie, one of the nurses who's worked here since I was probably a kid.

"I'm just here to talk with Lindsay for a few minutes," I answer Debbie.

Lindsay turns, giving me her attention now that she's off the phone. Her face lights up when she sees me, her smile hitting me square in the chest.

"Hey!" she says, standing and giving me a short hug. "What are you doing here?" she asks.

"Just came by to see you and to ask you something," I tell her and think *here goes nothing*.

"Oh yeah?" she questions. "What's that?"

"Can I take you out tomorrow night on a date?"

"Ooh," I hear coming from the other nurses behind Lindsay. "She says yes," one of them calls out, and Lindsay's shoulders start to shake from her laughter.

After turning to look at her coworkers, I can only imagine the look she gives them. She turns back to me. Her cheeks are a tad bit rosy from the blush that has crept onto them. "I'd love to go on a date with you tomorrow night," she tells me as her coworkers all hoot and make a ruckus behind her.

68

They're almost as bad as a firehouse full of guys. *Almost.*

"Perfect, I'll pick you up at five."

"Okay." She gives me a huge smile. "Any clues on what we'll be doing, so I know how to dress?" she asks.

"Nothing super fancy, dress in whatever you're most comfortable in."

"That I can do."

"I guess I should let you get back to work; I'll see you tomorrow night."

"See you then," she says before I pull her in for a quick hug. I release her after just a few seconds. If I didn't end the hug when I did, I don't know that things would have stayed PG. I take a few steps back, still holding eye contact with Lindsay. "Hey, Tucker," she says, my name all breathy like, and my damn brain goes to what she'd sound like calling my name out when I make her come.

"Yeah?" I finally remember to reply.

"Watch out behind you," she says, a smirk on her lips as I back into a column that I forgot was behind me.

"See you tomorrow," I reiterate. Thankfully, I don't completely make a fool of myself by crashing and burning after running into the wall. I do, however, turn and walk straight for the door.

I head to pick up Paisley from Lilly, and then to my parents' place.

"Nona!" Paisley calls out when we walk through the door.

"There's my princess!" Mom calls out as she pokes her head around the corner. "I'm in the kitchen; come help me with the cookies," she tells Paisley.

"Dad's in the living room watching football," Mom says to me as Paisley runs to the kitchen after we've removed our shoes.

I head into the kitchen, stopping first to kiss my mother on the cheek and sneak a spoonful of the cookie batter, before I grab two beers from the fridge and then head out to the living room to join my dad.

"How's it going?" he asks, kicked back in his recliner. I pop the top on one of the beers, holding it up for him. He takes it, and I do the same with the second one for me before I sit down on the couch facing the TV.

"Pretty damn good," I tell him before I take a drink of the cold beer.

"You're going to have to expand on that for me." He chortles.

"Just been a good day, that's all."

"Who is she?" he asks; not much has ever gotten past Pops.

"What makes you think there's a woman involved?" I ask.

"A few things, actually," he says, tipping his beer bottle at me. "First off, you practically came bouncing in here; secondly, I hear you had dinner with someone at the firehouse last night, and thirdly, you've just been a little different lately."

Well, hell. "Lindsay Blackwood," I tell him. No reason to hide anything about who's got me wound up like a bull in a shoot, ready to be released with a rider on his back.

"Nice girl, good family, and ties to the community. She works over at the hospital, yes?" Dad questions.

"Yep, a nurse in the ER," I confirm. "We've spent some time together as friends, lately, and there's been some sparks. Something that I'm interested in feeling out, so I asked her out, and we've got a date tomorrow night."

"What are your plans for said date?" Dad asks.

"That, I've still got to figure out. All I know, so far, is that I'm picking her up at five."

"You'd better get things figured out." Dad laughs at my expense.

"No shit, Sherlock," I deadpan. "I was thinking of driving over to the fall festival at the fairgrounds. We can take in the food and vendors, hang out and listen to the free concert that will be going on."

"Is Paisley going to be with you?" he asks.

"I was hoping that she could stay the night here?" I ask, knowing that my parents, nor Paisley, would turn down the chance to have a sleepover together.

"Of course. Your mom will be ecstatic."

"What will I be ecstatic about?" Mom asks, her and Paisley carrying a plate of warm cookies into the living room and handing them over to Dad and me.

"That Princess Paisley gets to have a sleepover with us tomorrow night," Dad tells both of them. I hadn't yet brought it up to Paisley but knew that she'd have no issues with it.

"Yes!" Paisley cheers, jumping up and down, throwing her fist into the air.

I snag one of the hot cookies, stuffing it into my mouth. The melted chocolate hits my tongue, and I have to hold back a groan. My mom's always been a fantastic cook and baker. I swear she could put Betty Crocker to shame. Everyone just loves whatever she makes.

"So, what's up tomorrow night?" Mom asks, sitting down on the couch next to me.

"I've got a date with Lindsay," I tell Mom, filling her in.

"About time you went after a wholesome girl," Mom says. She's asked me a few times over the years when I was going to settle down and possibly give her and Dad more grandkids. Seeing as I'm an only child, I'm their only shot at grandkids, and while I know they'd be happy as can be with just Paisley, they'd like to spread the love around to some more, if they come along.

"Daddy," Paisley says my name all-seriously, or as seriously as a four-year-old can.

"Paisley," I state her full name, so she knows she's got my attention.

"What's a date?" she asks, looking up at me from where she's been splashing around in the bath.

"It's when two people go somewhere together, like to dinner or to the movies. Like what Mommy and Mike do sometimes," I explain to her as best as I can.

"Who's Lindsay?" she asks, all inquisitive.

"One of Daddy's friends. I've known her since I was your age," I tell her as I pull my phone out and open up Facebook. I find Lindsay's page and tap on her profile picture, making it fill my screen. I flip the phone around, showing Paisley who I'm talking about. I know that they've met before; I just can't place when and where that would have been. Probably at some town function.

"She's pretty," Paisley comments.

"She is," I agree with my daughter. I help her wash her hair before rinsing her off and getting her out of the tub and ready for bed.

"How are you liking pre-school?" I ask once she's brushed her teeth and is picking out a book for me to read to her before she falls asleep. Lilly thought that it might be a good thing for us to try with her this year, especially with the new baby at their house, plus, it will just help with the transition to kindergarten next fall.

"I's love it! We get to do art and play, and my teacher, Ms. Kristen, is so nice," she rambles on.

"I'm glad that you love it," I tell her, patting the bed next to where I'm already sitting, waiting on her to join me. She hands me the book and crawls up on the bed. I get her all tucked in and then dive into reading to her. With the book finished, I kiss her goodnight, her little eyes hardly staying open as I do.

"Night, Daddy, loves you," she says just as I stand up.

"Love you, too, baby girl."

———

WITH PAISLEY DROPPED OFF AT MY PARENTS' HOUSE FOR her sleepover, I head home to get ready to pick up Lindsay. I've got two hours, so plenty of time to get my truck cleaned out, showered, and dressed before I have to leave to be at her house by five.

As I'm driving through town back to my place, I go by

the local florist, and the idea strikes me to stop and get a bundle for Lindsay. Thankfully, there's no one behind me, so I slam on my brakes in time to pull into their parking lot.

"How can I help you today?" the older lady behind the counter asks after I've entered the shop.

"I just need a bouquet of flowers," I tell her, politely.

"Any specific occasion?" she asks, coming out from behind the counter.

"A first date," I tell her, and she leads me over to one of the coolers holding already assembled bouquets.

"Do any of these catch your eye?" she asks. "Otherwise, you can select specific flowers from the loose bins, and I can arrange something special for you."

I know absolutely nothing about flowers, outside of women love them, and that roses are what they usually want on Valentine's Day. I look at the different options, finally settling on one that isn't the biggest arrangement but isn't the smallest by any means, either.

"Oh, that one's perfect!" the lady says as I remove it from the cooler. "Let me get you a box to set the vase in while driving." She disappears into the back room, coming back out a moment later with a box. She places the vase in it before ringing me up. I toss in a box of chocolates they have by the register from a local chocolate shop. I guess I'm going big or going home with this date.

I head home, flowers and chocolates secured in my truck. Once home, I quickly clean it out. I try to keep it clean, but a few wrappers and, of course, crumbs get in the back seat from Paisley eating in here on occasion.

An hour later, I've showered, shaved, and am standing in front of my closet in a pair of boxer briefs, trying to decide just what to wear tonight. I told Lindsay to keep it casual, so I need to do the same, plus, we're going to be outside for most of the night. I pull out a pair of shorts and a polo. Nothing too fancy, but also not just a junk T-shirt, either.

Once dressed, I check the time, and I've still got ten minutes to spare before I've got to leave. I check my wallet to make sure I've got cash for the fall festival. Not all of the vendors are set up to take debit cards, so cash is needed for tonight. I slip my wallet in my back pocket, grab my keys and cell, and head out to my truck. I only have forty bucks in my wallet, so I head out and hit up an ATM before driving over to Lindsay's house.

I park in her driveway, shutting my truck off and grabbing the flowers and chocolates. I make my way up to her front door, taking in the flowers that adorn her porch. She's got a cute little place, here. I rap my knuckles against the door as I patiently wait for her to answer.

"Hey," she says, smiling at me.

"Evening," I greet, trying my best to bring my southern charm front and center. "These are for you." I hand over the flowers and chocolates.

"These are gorgeous!" Lindsay exclaims as she takes the bouquet from me. She brings it to her nose, drawing in a large breath of the flowers. "And they smell amazing! Thank you so much." Lindsay opens her door even wider, allowing me to step inside behind her as she takes the flowers over to her counter.

"How was your day?" I ask, standing just inside the door.

"It was good, and yours?" she asks, coming back over to where I'm standing.

"Good, spent the morning and afternoon with Paisley until it was time to drop her off at my parents' house. She's having a sleepover with them tonight."

"Aww, I bet they'll have fun. Sorry that our date made you miss out on one of your nights with her."

"It's okay; I knew that she'd be just as happy at my parents' house as she is at mine. She's adjusting a little better to having a baby brother at Lilly's, as well," I tell her, thinking back to a few weeks ago when Paisley was having some difficulties with the transition to having a new sibling. "You ready to go?" I ask as Lindsay comes to a stop a foot or so in front of me. I realize I'm still holding the box of chocolates, so I hold them out, first. "These are also for you." I offer them over.

"How'd you know these were my favorite?" she asks, a little shock lacing her voice.

"Just a lucky guess." I smirk. "That, and they were next to the register at the florist, so really you have them to thank. Perfect product placement," I quip, but also make a mental note that they're her favorite. That's a good nugget of information to have for later on.

"Well, thank you," she says, placing them on a little table near her front door. "I'll enjoy those later. Now, where are you taking me?" she asks, and I open the door, holding out an arm for her to walk in front of me. I step aside once it's closed so that she can lock up, then offer up my arm for her to hold as I escort her to my truck. I break our connection once we reach it so that I can open the passenger door for her. I reach in and toss the box that held the flowers into my back seat, then offer my hand to help her climb up. I, apparently, will do anything to have her skin touching mine.

Once Lindsay is securely in the truck, I shut the door, jogging around the front and hopping into the driver's seat. "We're headed to the fall festival, if that sounds okay with you," I answer her question from before.

"Sounds perfect," she agrees. "I've been wanting to make it over, but didn't know when I'd be able to."

"Well, I'm glad it worked out, then." I chuckle.

We make small talk on the fifteen-minute drive over to the fairgrounds. With the nice weather, the festival is packed, especially with it being a Saturday night. I follow the signs to where parking is available, and we make our way up to the gates. I grab our tickets, and away we go.

"What are you in the mood to eat first?" I ask, placing my hand on Lindsay's back as we walk through the crowds.

She laughs. "I like how you specified *first*, like you already know we won't be indulging in just one thing tonight."

"It just isn't possible to come here and *not* eat your way through the place. Isn't that what fairs are all about?" I ask, leaning in a bit closer to talk next to her ear, so she's sure to hear me. With the growing crowds, it's a little hard to hear one another.

"Gah!" she exclaims, holding her hand up in the air. "I don't know what to pick, let's do a lap around, and then we can decide; how's that sound?" she asks, leaning right back into me.

"Like the perfect plan," I confirm. I slide my hand into hers, linking our fingers together as we walk around, checking things out. We each point out booths we want to check out at some point, but right now, we're on a mission to figure out our food game plan.

8

"I don't think I can eat one more bite," I tell Tucker as I push the basket of fresh curly fries closer to him. "I'm stuffed."

"Well, in your defense, we have eaten our way through this place." He snags another curly fry and drags it through the puddle of ketchup before popping it into his mouth. "But I agree, I'm done." He gathers what's left and tosses them in one of the large barrel trash cans set up around the tables.

"Want to go find a drink and go listen to music, or we could go grab some ride tickets and go up on the Ferris wheel," he suggests.

"I absolutely hate heights," I warn him. "So, I'm not sure you'd want to take me up on that thing."

"Oh, come on, it isn't that bad, plus, you'd have me to hold on to." He winks at me.

"You make a tempting argument, but I'm still not sure about getting on that thing."

"We can think about it, maybe go up once the sun fully sets, and all the lights come on."

"I'll think about it." I give him that, at least. The idea of snuggling close to him is *very* tempting, but the thought of losing the contents of my stomach all over him is definitely not.

"All right, let's go find a drink or two and then head over to the stage and listen to the music."

"Sounds perfect," I agree and stand from the picnic table. I toss the napkin I was holding, then slide my hand into Tucker's outstretched one. He's held my hand most of the evening, and I can admit that I like the feeling.

We find the beer tent, and he grabs two. He's insisted on paying for everything tonight, not that I expect it, at all. He almost glared at me once, when I attempted to pull out my wallet when I was buying a funnel cake earlier.

"I see an open space over there," I tell him, pointing at an empty section on the bleachers.

"Lead the way, beautiful," he comments, handing over one of the beers and then linking our fingers back together. I walk with him right on my heels until we reach the area. He waits to sit down until I take a seat, choosing to sit on the bench directly behind me. Once seated, he pulls me back until my back is against his front. I melt into him, enjoying the contact our bodies are making. His warmth seeps through my T-shirt but sends tingles of awareness down my spine.

We sway along to the music as we sit here, drinking our beers and just enjoying the entertainment on stage. This festival always brings in such amazing local talent, my cousin used to play this very stage each and every year until she made it big after winning the TV show she was on.

By the time the current band finished up, the sun has finally set, and the grounds are lit up by all the neon lights from the booths and the rides. We make our way out of the grandstand and back into the rows of booths. "What do you say about that Ferris wheel now?" Tucker asks, pulling me to a stop in front of him as we stand off to the side of the crowd of people. He's tucked his fingers into two of the belt loops on my jeans and pulled me in close. I place a palm against his chest, feeling the pounding of his heart against my fingers. I suck my bottom lip in between my teeth, biting it as I contemplate his offer. Here I am, twenty-six years old, out on a first date and pondering something that I probably had to consider when I was sixteen and at this very fair with my high school boyfriend at the time.

Tucker cups my cheek, his thumb sliding across my lip, pulling my bottom lip from my teeth. "I won't let anything happen to you," he says, his words a promise to protect me.

"Okay, let's do it," I tell him, finally giving in. The look of shock on his face tells me that he really didn't think that I'd go for it.

"Let's go!" he bellows, then tugs me toward the ticket booth. The crowds are thick, mostly with teenagers out after dark and enjoying the fun this Saturday night has brought to our ordinary sleepy town. It takes us a few minutes to get up to the booth, but once we do, Tucker buys enough tickets for us to go on the one ride.

"Have you ever gone on this?" Tucker asks once we're in line for the Ferris wheel.

"Once, I was sixteen. I hated every second of it and ended up puking when we got off. So be warned now that this might not end well," I warn, those thoughts of doubt creeping back in.

"I'll hold your hair back for you if that happens. Puke doesn't phase me one bit. Either does blood," he quips.

"You might not be saying that when it's in your lap," I deadpan.

"Still wouldn't be the worst thing that has happened to me. Do you not remember what I do for a living?"

"Fight fires and rescue kittens out of trees for little old ladies?" I quip.

"Yeah, we'll go with that answer." He laughs as we move closer to the front of the line.

"Do you enjoy your job?" I ask.

"Absolutely. I wouldn't want to do anything else. I dreamed of following in my dad's footsteps since I understood what it was he did every day."

"It's good to have such passion for your job."

"What about you? Do you enjoy working in the ER?"

"I love it. Like you, I knew from an early age that I wanted to help people, and nursing just kind of worked. I didn't really know what department or specialty I wanted to work in until I started clinicals. The ER is like nothing else. The constant changing, you never know what you're going to get kind of atmosphere keeps you on your toes and moving. Very rarely do we ever have much downtime, and the shifts we do, it's almost like the calm before the storm. None of us like it when that happens because it's usually followed by complete chaos."

"I understand that thinking. When we've gone too long between calls at the firehouse, we all dread that next one because it's usually a big one."

"Have you decided on the dog decision for Paisley's birthday?" I ask, changing the subject.

"I haven't. I really need to decide one way or another, soon. Her birthday is this week."

"Aww, are you guys doing anything special?" I ask.

"A party next weekend. Would you like to come?" he offers.

"Oh, I wouldn't want to intrude."

"You wouldn't be an intrusion, plus, I invited you."

"What are you guys doing?"

"She wanted one of those bounce castles, so I rented one to be set up in the backyard. Lilly and I have always just done one joint celebration for her every year, so everyone will be at one party. Just grilling up some hot dogs and hamburgers and letting the kids run around and play. Nothing super fancy, just a family-friendly party, plus some cake and ice cream, at some point. We're starting at noon, so if you are free and want to stop by, then I'd love to have you."

"Thanks, I'll see what's going on and maybe stop by," I tell him as we reach the front of the line—the worker holding the gate open for us to take a seat. I cautiously take a seat, then latch myself to Tucker's side as soon as he's next to me. The carnie locks the gate contraption that goes in front of us, then presses a button, causing us to move so they can unload and load the next one.

"I've got you." Tucker's deep sexy voice fills my ear. He places one arm around me, tugging me even closer to his side as his other hand holds mine. His lips are next to my ear as he does his best to keep my nerves at bay with his calming words. "We're just moving a little at a time, nothing to be scared of right now," he says, and I open my eyes up slightly. We've only moved enough space for them to unload and re-load two others. I keep my eyes open, even as we move up another spot. "See, you've got this. Just look at me if you need to."

"How can you be so calm?" I finally get out.

"Heights don't scare me, babe. I climb ladders every day, walk along rooflines of buildings that are on fire."

"And you're crazy," I quip.

"Not crazy, just live for the adrenaline rush that being out on calls brings me."

"Ohhh, shit!" I call out as the Ferris wheel starts moving again, this time not stopping after just twenty or so feet. As we creep toward the very top, I feel my stomach roll, but try and focus on keeping my breathing steady and regular.

"I've got you," Tucker says again into my ear, his lips practically touching my neck. His breath on my skin definitely has me distracted as we descend back to the ground and then lift right back up as we circle around. Tucker's lips suck, lighting at the skin just below my ear. My pulse picks up at the contact as lust fills my veins. I sink my free hand into his hair, pulling his lips from my neck, and crush my lips against his. I melt into the connection. His tongue slides along the seam of my lips, and I open for him instantly. He shifts slightly, not like we can sit much differently in this Ferris wheel cart, but he somehow deepens the kiss, making me forget about my surroundings.

"Time's up, love birds," the carnie's voice calls out, and Tucker and I break apart instantly. My cheeks are hot from my embarrassment. Tucker hops off, tugging my hand behind him as we exit and run down the ramp. A giggle comes barreling out, and I can't stop the laugh from being caught making out like teenagers by the carnie.

"That wasn't so bad, now, was it?" Tucker asks once we've cleared the exit ropes and are now standing out in the open, the crowds of people milling around. He pulls me back into his arms, my front flush with his. He sinks both hands into my hair, pulling my face back to being in front of his.

"It definitely was better than the last time I rode the thing," I say against his lips, just as he kisses me once again.

Butterflies fill my stomach as we stand here kissing, our surroundings melting away once again. The bells and music blaring out from all the games and rides are just a faint noise in the background. I can feel the effect our kiss is having on Tucker's body as his erection presses into my belly. What I wouldn't do to be able to touch him right now, but unless I want to get carted off for indecent exposure, this isn't the time or place to be copping a feel.

"Get a room!" I hear a voice call out, causing us to break apart. He's got a shit-eating grin tugging at his lips. His forehead rests against mine as he sucks in a deep breath.

"Ready to get out of here?" he asks, standing to his full height, a moment later. His thumb wipes across my kiss-swollen lips before he takes a step back.

"Yeah, let's go," I reply. Linking our fingers back together, we walk side-by-side out of the fair and to his truck.

The drive back to my place is quiet, except for the sound coming from the radio. Once on the road, Tucker placed his hand on my thigh and hasn't moved it since. He pulls into my driveway, and the butterflies are back. Do I invite him in? Do we call it a night here at the truck? At the door? *Why am I overthinking this?*

"Would you like—" I start to say just as he starts to talk.

"I'm not ready—" he's saying.

"Sorry, you first," I tell him.

"No, you go first," he insists.

"Would you like to come in?" I finish my question.

"Yes," he chuckles as he replies. "I was about to tell you that I wasn't ready for our night to end."

"Well, then, I guess we're on the same page," I tell him as I open my door and jump down from his truck. He follows me up to my front stoop, waiting behind me as I pull out my keys and unlock the door. His fingertips graze over the skin on my neck as he pushes my hair out of the way, his lips finding bare skin. My fingers shake as I turn the lock, and then handle, and push the door open. I step out of his embrace, immediately missing the feel of his lips against my skin. He follows me inside, turning to shut the door behind him.

Tucker tugs me into his arms, turning me, so I'm

facing him. "I don't want to rush you into this, but I need to know what you want tonight. I'm not looking for just a one-night romp in the sheets, Lindsay," he tells me, and the look of desire that floods his blue eyes tells me so much more than his words do, at this moment.

"I, I don't know, Tucker. Let's just see where things go," I suggest. I can't just word vomit all over him that I want a relationship; I want the white picket fence, two kids, and dog life. We just went on our first official date. It doesn't matter. I've known this man practically my entire life; if I was to lay out everything I'm looking for right now, he'd be out the door faster than he arrived.

"Okay," he agrees, backing me up against the wall and kissing me once again. This toe-curling kiss is somehow hotter than any of the other ones we've had tonight. Maybe it is the fact we're actually alone, with no chance of being interrupted. Perhaps it's because the sexual tension has built up not only from tonight but the last few weeks. I don't know what it is, but I'm sure as hell not complaining.

Tucker keeps me pinned against the wall, his thigh separating my legs and applying the perfect amount of pressure to my aching core. I might have even ground myself against him a few times, and I'm not even ashamed of it. His lips find their way down my jaw and back to my throat. The light scruff on his face tickling my skin as he moves his lips around. He sucks lightly at my throbbing pulse before pulling back and looking at me, his eyes so lust drunk.

"If I don't stop now, I don't know that I'll be able to

hold back from taking you into your room and stripping you down and fucking you all night long," he growls.

"Mhmm..." I moan. The images flashing through my mind from his words have me squirming against his thigh again.

"And tell me *why* that's a bad idea?" I ask, my breath a little shaky.

"Fuck, Linds," he says, bringing his forehead to mine. "You can't say shit like that and expect me not to haul you over my shoulder." He pulls back, standing to his full height, which causes his thigh to no longer be between my legs. I immediately miss the heat and pressure it was providing.

"I say we throw caution to the wind and find a flat surface," I tell him. I don't know where this boldness is coming from, but dammit, I'm a grown woman and can ask for sex if I damn well want to.

"You sure? I don't want you regretting anything come the daylight hours," he says, looking me over.

"Are you turning down sex?" I ask, a little shocked.

"For tonight, yes. I don't think we should rush things. I think we should have another date before we take that next step; I don't want to be a mistake, Linds. I want to be more."

"I want to see what can come of whatever this is between the two of us. I know who you are deep down, I know your values and the type of man you truly are, and I want that man in my life."

"How about you show me to the couch, and we can watch a movie before I head home for the night? I just want to hold you for a while longer."

9

LINDSAY

"WHAT TIME ARE WE MEETING THE GUYS AT THE BAR?" Allison asks while I fix my eye makeup. I've got her on speakerphone so that I can use both hands.

"An hour," I tell her as I swipe the mascara wand across my lashes a second time.

"Do you want to swing by and pick me up or just meet there?" she asks.

"I can pick you up; that way, when you go home with Lee, you don't have to leave your car at Joe's for everyone to know the next morning that you didn't drive home."

"Who's to say I'm going home with Lee?" she questions, trying hard to feign her innocence in that assumption.

"I'd bet drinks for our next girls' night that you go home together," I tell her as I toss the mascara into my makeup bag sitting on the counter.

"Nope. Not taking any bets." I can totally hear the smile in her voice.

"What about your car? I have a feeling you could

leave with Tucker just as easily as I'd leave with Lee," Allison asks.

"I guess I'll just drive myself home, and he can follow me," I tell her, shrugging my shoulders, even though she can't see me.

"Hold on, I'm getting a call from Lee. I'll be right back," she says, and my phone goes silent after she clicks over to take his call. I turn side to side, checking out my reflection from as many angles as I can to make sure that I look okay from all sides. Approving of my simple yet sexy look, I grab my cell and head for the kitchen.

"Okay," Allison's voice comes back over my speaker. "I'm back and change of plans."

"What do you mean, change of plans?" I question.

"The guys, apparently, were thinking ahead as we were, and they're picking us up. Lee said Tucker will be at your place in about thirty, and Lee will be at mine in about the same amount of time. Then we'll meet at the bar."

"I guess that works and solves the car issue," I say. I fill a glass with water, starting early with the hydration so that I don't regret tonight's drinks tomorrow.

"I'm going to go so I can finish getting ready! See you soon."

"Bye," I call out before the line goes dead. Since I'm ready early, I take my water and go plop myself down on the couch while I wait for Tucker to pick me up.

I look outside and the sun is setting, lighting up the sky in some beautiful colors, so I decide to go sit out on the porch and enjoy it. He should be here in the next ten minutes, so I take advantage of that time. I stand on my porch, my back to the open air, and snap a selfie with the colors of the sky lighting up behind me. I add it to my Instagram account, *Beautiful night in Monroe!* I captioned the post and hit submit. I take a seat on the rocking chair on my porch, just watching as the colors change as the sun sets in the distance.

A few minutes later, I hear the rumble of Tucker's truck coming down the road. I stay on the rocking chair while he pulls into my drive, parking in the spot nearest to my front door.

"Hey, gorgeous," he greets as he makes his way over to the steps. "You ready to go?"

"I am; how was your day?" I ask, making small talk as I stand and join him at the bottom of the stairs. He slides an arm around my waist, pulling me flush against his front.

"It's better now," he growls, his face going to my neck. A shiver slides down my spine as his breath hits my skin and then his lips. "I've missed the fuck out of you," he whispers into my ear before moving and claiming my mouth in a demanding kiss that leaves my body humming in anticipation of what's to come later tonight. After he turned me down for sex the other night, I've had to take matters into my own hands a few times, but it was nothing compared to what I'm sure he can do.

"Damn," I whisper against his lips. "If that's the kind of greeting I'm going to get, you'd best be stopping over here every day," I joke with him. I step away quick to lock the door and grab my wristlet and phone from where I'd placed them next to the rocking chair.

"Don't tempt me, woman," he says, snagging my hand

and tugging me behind him as we head for his truck. "If we don't leave now, I don't know if we ever will," he grunts out as we close the distance to his truck.

"You owe me some dancing," I remind him, tapping his nose once we come to a stop next to the passenger door. I press a quick kiss to his cheek, then step back so he can open the door. I know he'd be pissed if I attempted to do it myself.

"That I do," he agrees as I get settled into the seat. I watch as he rounds the front of his truck and then settles into his seat and buckles up before we back out of the driveway.

"WHO WANTS ANOTHER ROUND?" LEE CALLS OUT, LOOKING at the table before he heads for the bar. Joe's behind it tonight, just like every ladies' night that I've ever been to, I believe. He comes back a few minutes later with a pitcher of beer and starts filling everyone's glasses.

"Only half a glass for me, please," I tell him before he fills it to the top. Tucker slides behind me, having just come back from the bathroom. It's hot in the bar with how busy it is tonight, but the moment his hand slips along my hip and his thumb finds bare skin between my shirt and jeans, a shiver makes its way down my spine. I've noticed my body responds to his touches like that a lot. We're like fire and ice. I'm attracted to his flame, but the moment our skin makes contact, it's like ice, but in a very good way.

"You want to dance?" he whispers in my ear a few

minutes later. I've finished off my half glass of beer as we've talked with everyone standing around our table, or more so, listened to their conversation. My mind was focused more on the feel of his thumb tracing lazy circles on my hip and what I wouldn't do for that hand to slip entirely under my top or below the waistband of my jeans.

"Yes," I answer, letting my head press against his shoulder behind me.

"We're going back out," Tucker says to the group at large. Before anyone can reply, he's leading me out on the floor just as "From This Moment" by Shania Twain and Bryan White fills the speakers. I used to love this old song, and I let the words filter into my mind as I let Tucker sway us in a small circle. I hear him quietly singing a few of the lyrics of the song along with Bryan and Shania. His words are hardly even loud enough for me to hear completely.

The song ends, but he holds on tight. The way we stop on the dance floor, I can see our group of friends, and catch a few of Tucker's truck mates giving him a look as if they're asking if we can get any closer out here on the dance floor.

"Everyone is staring at us," I tell him, bringing my attention back to Tucker and not our friends.

"We could put these rumors to rest and really give them something to talk about," he tells me before cupping my face and claiming my mouth. I can faintly hear the catcalls from all our friends, and the calls of "it's about time" from them, as well.

I can't hold it in any longer, breaking the kiss so I can

laugh at their antics and the show we're putting on out here on the dance floor.

"So, what now?" I ask, placing my hands against Tucker's chest and looking up at him.

"You're mine," he growls. "From this moment," he tells me, quoting the lyrics from the song we just danced to.

THE DRIVE BACK TO MY PLACE TAKES ONLY MINUTES BUT feels like an hour. All the light touches building up to that kiss on the dance floor, and Tucker claiming me in front of our friends and everyone else in the bar has me hoping that he's on board with staying the night tonight and losing our clothes. I don't know how much more build-up I can take.

Tucker cuts the engine once he's parked in my driveway, then turns to look at me. "What are we doing tonight, sweetheart?" His slight southern accent is coming out in his question.

"I don't know, you tell me." I toss the decision right back at him. He's the one that put the brakes on things last weekend. While I was a tad bit disappointed at the time, I know it was for the best. There's no need to jump into sex. It should be something special, and it is okay to wait for a few dates to take that step.

"I know what I want to do, but I want to know what *you* want. There's no pressure from me for anything you're not comfortable with."

"I know," I tell him, knowing damn well that even if I

told him to take me inside and fuck me, and then changed my mind once we were naked, he'd back off without a second word. That's just the kind of man Tucker is. "Let's head inside. Maybe have a nightcap and see where that leads us," I suggest. That leaves things open to more happening, or we might just fall asleep on the couch together.

"Okay," Tucker agrees to my suggestion and hops out of his truck. I open my door, waiting for him to come around, taking his hand to help me jump down. I lead the way up to my house, almost getting a déjà vu feeling from our previous date.

"What would you like to drink?" I ask, tossing my keys onto the rack just inside my door.

"A beer is fine if you have one," Tucker says, toeing off his boots.

He looks mighty fine tonight in his tight but not skin-tight Wranglers that show off his ass, cowboy boots, and a button-up shirt. Looking like the southern gentleman he is.

I grab him a beer and me a glass of water and meet him back out in the living room. I hand over the beer, taking a drink of my water before setting it down on the end table. I sit down on the couch, patting the cushion next to me for Tucker to join me. He does so, plopping down next to me, his arm going around my shoulder and pulling me in closer to his side. I end up rotating until I'm lying on my back, my head in his lap, and looking up at him. His fingers start to slide through my hair, and the feeling has me groaning in pleasure.

"You'd best be careful moaning like that, especially

with your head in my lap," he warns, and I smirk just as another groan escapes.

"You could make me moan a whole lot more if you'd just take me to bed," I throw out there. I don't know if it's Tucker that makes me so bold or the alcohol or the combination of both, but I'm apparently not afraid of asking for what I want tonight.

"I don't know what I did to deserve someone like you in my life, but fuck if I'm going to pass this opportunity by," he says, just as he stands and swoops me up on his shoulder, fireman style, of course, and carries me down the hall. "What bedroom is yours?" he asks, and I can't help but laugh at his quickness and the way he's got me slung over his shoulder.

"The second door on the left," I say, slapping his ass as he quickly walks down the short hall. He deposits me on the end of the bed, and I take a quick peek around my room to make sure that I didn't leave it in a disaster zone after trying on multiple things before settling on my outfit.

He stands, bracing his arms on each side of me. "I've got a few rules for tonight," he says, dropping a kiss to my shoulder.

"Do you now?" I ask, quirking a brow at him.

"First, you say stop, and we stop," he says, kissing my cheek. "Second, no matter how far we go tonight, I want you in my arms all night." He kisses my other cheek. "Third, you let me make you breakfast in the morning and then spend the day with Paisley and me tomorrow. I want her to get comfortable with you around and vice versa. She inquired what a date was after she heard me telling my parents about our date last weekend."

"Okay. I agree with these three rules." I kiss his lips lightly. "Do I get to have any of my own rules?" I ask, trying to see how much I can push him.

"Of course, let me hear them," he says, standing up straight, his hands landing on his hips. I drop my eyes to the bulge in his jeans, and my mouth waters at the thought of getting him out of said clothing.

"First," I start, slightly mocking him. "You're going to drop those jeans, the shirt, as well, and whatever you've got under them," I tell him, flicking my eyes back up to his, the room dark except for the hall light that shines in, giving off just enough light so we can see one another. His pupils dilate a little more at my words. "Second, you're going to stand there while I suck your cock." I purposely slide my tongue along my bottom lip just to see what he does at my bold words, and am slightly disappointed when he doesn't start dropping his clothes. "Third," I begin to say but don't get to finish because his lips land against mine in a demanding kiss. His body presses into mine, taking me flat against the mattress.

My hands slide into his hair as he finds the bottom of my shirt. He pulls it up as his fingers glide up my skin. The feel of his calloused fingers causes my body to break out in goosebumps and send tingles down my spine. "You're going to be the death of me, and I haven't even been inside of you yet," he says against my lips after breaking our kiss.

I take the chance and pull my shirt off over my head. Tucker follows suit, shucking his own. I unbutton my jeans and start to shimmy them off my hips, deciding to leave my panties on for now. I slide the jeans down my legs, having to sit up so I can get them entirely off. I slide off the bed, tossing my shirt and jeans toward my laundry basket, then rounding the bed and flipping my bedside lamp on. The light floods the room in a low glow, giving us just enough light to see one another, but not so bright that it is distracting. I know some women prefer to have sex, especially with a new partner, in a dark room, but I want to see him. I might not have the tightest body around, but I'm also not ashamed of my healthy curves.

I look over at Tucker, still standing at the end of the bed; he's also down to just his boxer briefs, and damn do they hug him nicely. He's all sinewy muscles, tanned skin, and a few tattoos that I, all of a sudden, find myself wanting to trace. He drinks me in, standing now in only my bra and panties.

"You're beautiful, you know that, right?" he asks, the desire he's not hiding also evident in his voice.

"Thank you, I'd say the same for you, but men don't like to be called that, right?" I ask, trying to keep the moment light.

"I don't care what the hell you call me right now; as long as you aren't telling me to get out, I'm a happy man."

"Definitely not saying that," I tell him as I slowly start to close the distance between the two of us.

Once I'm standing just a few inches in front of him, I reach out and bring my palm to his chest. I trace the tattoo of Paisley's name across his heart. It's a beautiful script font surrounded by a few flowers.

My fingers leave his tattoo, drifting down his abs. I

love how his body reacts, twitching under my touch as my fingers ghost down his ridges. I don't miss the twitch of his cock in his boxer briefs, as they don't leave much to the imagination. I sink to my knees in front of him, pulling the elastic of his briefs down as I do. I look up at him as his cock springs free, making sure he's enjoying this as much as I am. I'm met with eyes that are so lust drunk that it spurs me on even more. I want nothing more than to bring this man to the edge of pleasure and make him fall over.

I run my fingernails up his thighs, appreciating how they quiver under my touch. His cock is hard and standing at attention. I wrap a fist around the base, giving him a quick squeeze just as I dart my tongue out and lick the bead of pre-cum from the tip. "Holy shit, Linds," he groans out, his fingers sinking into my hair as he gathers it out of my way and pulls it all into his fist. I lick around the head of his cock, then down the underside, before coming back up and sucking him fully into my mouth. My fist following my mouth up and down his shaft as I work him over. My tongue runs circles around his head, flicking the sensitive spots that I get the most reactions to. I hollow out my cheeks as I suck him until his cock is hitting my throat before I pull back, popping him out of my mouth. I keep my fist moving up and down as I catch my breath, watching his reaction.

"I think that's enough," he says, reaching down to pick me up by my armpits.

I continue to stroke his cock as he kisses me hard. His hands slide down my sides until he's cupping my ass. He lifts me up, and I have to let go of his cock as my legs wrap around his torso. The press of his hard shaft against my needy center sends shockwaves through my body.

Tucker breaks the kiss, bringing his face down my neck and to my chest. One of his hands slides up my back, finding the back of my bra, and a quick flick of his wrist, and my bra is falling off. I should probably be a little offended by how quickly he was able to unclasp my bra, but now is definitely not the time to unpack that tidbit. "Fuck, your tits are perfect," he says, licking at one of my nipples before he sucks it into his mouth. My head falls back, bringing my chest up and pushing it further into his face. He switches breasts, repeating everything on the other one.

He turns us so that the bed is behind me, then places me on it, my ass at about the edge of the mattress. My legs fall from being wrapped around him and rest on either side of his hips. He pulls up from lavishing my breasts, looking deeply into my eyes before he traces a fingertip from my lips, down my neck, and between my breasts. He continues sliding it down my torso, his lips occasionally following it as he drops kisses to my exposed skin. Each kiss causes my skin to pucker in goosebumps until his fingertip reaches my panties. "Can I take these off of you?" he asks, his voice deep and gritty.

His question almost catches me by surprise, but that's just the kind of man that Tucker is. He wants me to know that I'm in charge here. He might be the one to deliver the pleasure I'm about to experience, but I'm the one in control. "Yes," I answer him, nodding my head along with my words.

"Good girl," he praises me as he slips both hands into

the elastic and tugs them down my hips. I lift my ass up off the bed a few inches to help him. He quickly pulls them down my legs, tossing them over his shoulder once they've cleared my feet. He takes his fill of my now naked body. One of his hands ghosts up my leg and across my mound. I keep it trimmed and tidy. I've never liked the look or feel of going completely bare, but tidy is an absolute must.

"You're so wet and ready for me," he muses, his fingers easily sliding between my folds. He watches me, my reaction as he slips two fingers inside of me. My back bows off the bed, the intrusion of his fingers one I need more than I knew. He finds my g-spot, figuring out crazy fast how to make me almost fall apart at his touch. My eyes have fallen closed as I enjoy whatever pleasure he wants to deliver to me. I about come unglued when his mouth joins his fingers, and he sucks my clit into his mouth. His tongue is flicking it relentlessly until I'm crying out as my orgasm takes my body over the edge. My legs wrap around his head, holding him to my core for a few seconds as I explode. My body then going limp against the mattress.

He kisses the inside of my thighs as he pulls his fingers from my pussy. I immediately miss the fullness his fingers provided. He slides onto the bed, lying beside me, kissing random places on his way up. "Ready for more?" he asks once I've caught my breath.

"I think so, although I don't know if I can come again after that," I tell him honestly. I've never been one to come multiple times during sex. One time is usually it for me.

"Oh, trust me, baby. You'll be coming a few more times before I let you go to sleep tonight," he says all cockily. I can't help but laugh at him.

"Do you have a condom?" I think to ask; I don't have any here. Seeing as I don't really sleep around, I've never kept any at my place unless in a committed relationship with a man.

"I should have one in my wallet," he says, kissing my ribs before pushing himself off the bed and going in search of his shorts. He slips his wallet from his pocket and fishes around in it, pulling out one silver packet and tossing it to the bed.

"We've got one to last us, for now. I'll make sure to buy a box to leave here," he says before returning his wallet to his pocket, then dropping it back to the floor. He picks the packet back up, rips it open with his teeth, and rolls it down his shaft. His fingers go back to my center, making sure I'm still wet and ready for him. My legs fall open, accommodating the width of his hips as he slides between me. With his cock at my entrance, his lips find mine once again. "You good?" he asks, and at my nod, he thrusts inside me.

"Holy shit!" I cry as he fills me completely. I thought his fingers made me feel full, but they had nothing on his cock.

"Fuck," he growls, pulling out of me. "Did I hurt you?" he asks, the concern lacing his voice evident.

"No," I can't help but laugh. "I mean, there was a slight pinch of pain, but that was more due to the amount of time it's been since I last had sex, but it felt good, better than good, so please get back inside me," I ramble. I can't believe I'm rambling while Tucker hovers above me, his cock slick from being inside me.

"You're sure?" he asks, pressing a sweet kiss against my lips.

"Yes," I instruct him, reaching between us and aligning his cock back up with my entrance as I encourage him to slide back inside of me. He gives in, sliding back in, this time slowly rather than a fast thrust like last time. His slow thrusts are torturous. The slow buildup they cause. He finally increases his rhythm, finding a pace that we're both enjoying if the moans and inaudible words falling from our lips are any indications.

"I can't hold out much longer, Linds. I need you with me," he whispers into my ear. "You with me, baby?" he asks. I don't know how he's done it, but I am. My body is ready to explode once again. He presses his thumb to my clit, and I fall apart as he thrusts a few more times. He collapses on me, pinning me entirely to the mattress. The weight of his body on mine is a foreign feeling, but one that I'd happily take if it means mutual orgasms like he just delivered to both of us.

Once he's calmed his breathing, he slips from me, and I once again miss the fullness his body filled me with. He slides completely off the bed, looking around for where he can dispose of the condom, I'm sure.

"Bathroom is through that door," I tell him, pointing at my bathroom. He slides the condom off, tying it off as he makes his way into the bathroom. I lay in my complete blissed-out state, enjoying my orgasm drunkenness. I vaguely register the toilet flushing and the water turning on. I startle when a warm washcloth touches my skin as he places one against my core. He wipes me carefully before taking the washcloth back to the bathroom. I follow him, needing to pee before I can fall asleep.

Once I've finished my bathroom business, I find him lying in bed, his back propped up against the headboard as he scrolls the screen of his phone. He's got the blanket and sheet pulled back on my side, and it's covering his legs, the material pooling in his lap.

As I approach my side of the bed, he places his phone on the end table on that side, then rolls to face me. "I hope you don't mind that I made myself at home in your bed." He flashes me a panty-melting smile. "With your things on that side, I figured this one was open for me to claim."

"Did you now?" I ask, quirking my brow at him. He snakes an arm out, pulling me into the bed as he expertly rolls on top of me, effectively pinning me under his big body. I can't help but laugh at his antics.

"Don't make me tickle you," he warns through the smile that tugs at his lips playfully. This is the kind of ease I want in a partner.

"You tickle me, and you risk a knee to the balls," I warn. "I *do not* like being tickled, so you've been warned," I tell him, the humor draining from my voice.

"Okay," he says as he rolls us so we're facing one another, lying on our sides. He's still naked underneath the sheets, which makes me feel better, since I wasn't sure if I should slip some panties or a tank top back on now that we've had sex.

"Since we're out of condoms, for the time being, my plan of fucking you all night is out the window, but that doesn't mean I can't kiss you some more," he says before he does just that.

"I need to sleep," I finally tell him, pulling away from his delicious lips.

"I know, I need some sleep, too, if I have any chance of keeping up with Paisley tomorrow—I mean, later today," he says after looking at the clock over my shoulder.

"Do I even want to know what time it is?" I ask as I yawn.

"Probably not." He smiles, then presses another kiss to my lips. "Sleep, beautiful," he says, yawning himself. We snuggle in together, both of us adjusting a few times before we find a comfortable position before we both are claimed by sleep.

10

TUCKER

I watch as the rental company sets up the bounce house castle that Lilly and I rented for Paisley's party today. It fills up a large portion of my backyard, one of the reasons that I suggested we have the party here. I knew that it wouldn't leave much room for anything else in Lilly and Mike's yard. They were more than happy to have it here and not have to deal with the party prep at their house.

"Daddy," Paisley calls out as she joins me on the back deck.

"Yes, baby?" I reply, turning and swooping her up in my arms. Her little arm wraps around my neck, her little lips finding my cheek as she presses a kiss there. She's done that since forever, and I know that one day I'll miss that. One day she'll be too old to kiss her daddy on his cheek every chance she gets.

"Can I go bounce yet?" she asks, looking longingly at the bounce house as it swells up with air as the blowers go to work.

"Not quite yet. Once it is filled with air, the workers have to secure it to the ground so that it doesn't go flying in the air. But once they've done that, then you can."

"Will you bounce with me?" she asks.

"Sure will," I tell her as I hear a door shut out front. "Should we go see who's here?" I ask her, and she slides her way out of my arms and goes running down the deck and around the house. I'm close on her heels, checking to see who's arrived early.

"Nona, Papa!" Paisley calls out as my parents grab the presents from their back seat. They both have multiple items in their arms, damn grandparents going overboard again with the number of gifts they are spoiling her with.

"How's the birthday girl?" Mom asks, crouching down to Paisley's height to give her a hug and kiss.

"Good! Are these all for me?" she asks, looking at the pile of presents.

"Of course, who else would they be for?" Dad asks her.

Paisley just shrugs her shoulders and leads the way inside. We cleared a small table for presents to go on, and she shows them the way to that very spot. I placed the *one* gift I already picked up for her to have at her party to open when it's time. She's getting another present from me—I'm caving and buying a dog—but that won't happen until after her party. With Lindsay's help this past week, and a promise from my mom that she'll help when I'm at work, I did some research trying to decide the best type of dog to get. I stopped in at one of the rescues and found a lab that was a few years old, good with kids, and well trained. The old man who owned him suffered a stroke and had to move into a nursing home that wasn't pet-friendly, so he's been living with a foster family until a family came along that could adopt him. I've spent some time with him in the evenings and my days off and think that Paisley is going to love him. My plan is to take her over to meet him once the party is over, and as long as that meeting goes well, he'll come home with us. She's going to be over the moon, excited.

Before we know it, the party is going strong. Friends and family fill the yard and inside of my house. I look around and just take in all the people Paisley has in her life. She's one lucky kid, and, thankfully, she's taken to Lindsay being in our life reasonably well. I know she's used to sharing her mom with Mike, but I've never had a woman around when she's been at my place much. Even with the last few that I dated, I usually only saw them when Paisley was with her mom. So, knowing that I wanted Lindsay around, Paisley tells me everything I need to know about where this relationship is going or where I want it to go.

I look around, trying to see if I can find Lindsay. She said she'd be here by one, but I don't see her just yet. My mind starts to race that something has happened to make her late, but looking at my phone, I see that it's only just now one, so she isn't really all that late. Just as I'm sliding my phone back into my pocket, it vibrates with an incoming text.

Lindsay: I'm on my way, had to stop for gas, or I wouldn't have made it. See you soon!

Tucker: Drive safe, babe. See you when you get here.

Knowing that she's safe and on her way, I tuck my phone away and go to find my daughter. Today is all about her, after all.

"Did you have fun today?" Lindsay asks Paisley as she sits in the middle of the living room, surrounded by all her new presents. She's got so many new toys, games, clothes. It looks like the entire girls' section of Target puked in my living room.

"I did!" she exclaims. "It was so much fun."

"It was. Now, I've got one more present for you, but before we can go get it, we have to pick up your other presents. Think we can do that?" I ask Paisley.

"Another present?!" She perks up at that and looks at me.

"Yep, so let's get things put away, or at least picked up, so the living room floor isn't covered, and then we can go," I tell her, looking at the clock. I made arrangements with the foster family for us to come over at six for Paisley to meet Buckley.

"If you'd like, I can help you," Lindsay offers as she moves down to sit on the floor.

"Thanks!" Paisley tells her as she starts to pick things up.

"Maybe pile things up that you want to take to your

mom's house over here," Lindsay says, pointing to a spot under the front window.

"That's a good idea," Paisley agrees with her and does just that. I sit back, watching my daughter and girlfriend interact like they've been doing this forever, and I can see it. I can see more moments just like this, the three of us hanging out, Christmas mornings, birthdays and other holidays, and maybe, one day, another kid or two in the mix.

"How's that look, Daddy?" Paisley asks, drawing me out of my daydream. I look around and see that they've cleaned up everything. She's got a pile of the things she wants to take to Lilly's, and everything else is gone. I'm assuming she put them away in her room.

"Looks perfect. How'd you do that so fast?" I ask.

"Lindsay helped me!" she says, wrapping her little arms around Lindsay's neck.

"Thanks for that," I say to Lindsay.

"Of course. It was pretty easy once she decided what was staying and what was going with her tomorrow."

"So, how about we get loaded up in the truck and go find out what your last present is?" I ask.

"Yes!" Paisley exclaims and takes off for the front door, only slowing down long enough to put her shoes on and grab a light jacket from the hook.

"Thanks for all your help today." I snag Lindsay, wrapping my arms around her as I pull her into a hug before she can escape to put her shoes on, as well.

"Of course," she says, kissing me quickly before pulling away. "We'd better not keep her waiting." She chuckles as we hear Paisley call out to us from outside, asking when we're coming.

I can't help but laugh at my daughter's antics and the fact that we're being controlled by a five-year-old.

"You do realize we're allowing a five-year-old to control us, right?" I ask Lindsay.

"Like she hasn't ruled your world every day for the last five years?" she questions as she slips her feet into her boots.

"You've got me there," I tell her, slapping my hand against my heart.

I follow her out the door, stopping long enough to lock up. I make it over to the truck, checking to make sure that Paisley is appropriately secured in her seat in the back. She's learned how to buckle herself using the seat-belt. I might have had to hold back some tears when I realized my baby girl is growing up on me. I hardly blinked an eye, and she's five, I'm going to blink again, and she'll be walking down the aisle getting married.

Once we're all secured in the truck, I pull out, and we make our way over to the foster family's house.

"Before we go inside, this is someone else's house, so let's keep our manners a priority," I remind my daughter. I know she's going to be excited when she meets Buckley, and I don't want her to forget how to behave.

"Okay, Daddy," she agrees. "Why are we at someone's house?" she questions as we get out of the truck.

"You'll see in just a few minutes," I tell her as we approach the front door.

I rap my knuckles on the door, and we wait. A minute or so later, the door opens, and Rebecca, the foster mom, stands at the doorway, a smile on her face and Buckley by her side.

"You must be Paisley?" she asks excitedly. She knows what's going on and helped facilitate everything.

"I am," Paisley confirms.

"Well, this here is Buckley, and he's excited to meet you," Rebecca tells her. Paisley looks back at me, and her face lights up as it hits her that she's meeting a dog.

"We're getting a dog?" she asks, the excitement causing her little body to shake; she is so excited.

"Yep, well, as long as you and Buckley get along tonight, then yep, he'll get to come home with us," I explain.

"Why don't the three of you come in and spend some time with him, and then you can decide if he should go home with you," Rebecca suggests, opening the door wider so that we can all walk inside. I take it from her hands, allowing Paisley and then Lindsay to pass through the door first, and follow Rebecca into the living room.

Paisley goes right to hugging Buckley. He's so good with her, allowing her to play with him and his toys. Rebecca eventually suggests that we go out back, and Paisley takes a ball with, so that she can play fetch with him. The next hour blows by, and I watch as my daughter falls in love with the dog. It's a good thing, since I'd gotten kind of attached to him in the time I spent with him over the last couple of days.

Once Rebecca has observed our interaction to suffice the requirements of the rescue, she signs off on the paperwork, and Buckley is now ours! We load up his things in my truck, and he settles in perfectly next to Paisley's booster seat in the back. Looking at the two of them, you'd never know they just met a little over two hours ago.

We get home, Paisley jumping out of the truck with Buckley right with her. They take off for the backyard while Lindsay and I unload the things that Rebecca sent us home with. I'd already picked up a large bag of the type of food he's used to eating, and she sent us with his bowls, leash, a basket full of toys, his bed, and a crate that he's used to. We get it all brought into the house, and I figure out the best place to put his bed and crate.

"I think we should put his bed in Paisley's room, I don't think that you're going to be able to separate them, at least tonight," Lindsay suggests.

"You're probably right," I tell her, looking out the back door at them playing fetch in the backyard. The sun has set, so they're playing by the light of the moon and the lights on the backside of the house. "It's time to come in and get ready for bed," I call out. Looking at the clock, I see that it's already an hour past Paisley's bedtime. Good thing it's the weekend, and we don't have to be up early tomorrow.

"Daddy, can Buckley sleep in my room?" Paisley asks as they both enter the house. I can't help but laugh; Lindsay must be a mind reader.

"Yep, Lindsay even put his bed in your room already," I tell her.

"Thank you!" She twirls in excitement.

"You're welcome," Lindsay tells her, laughing at her antics.

"How about you go get ready for bed quick," I suggest.

"Okay," Paisley agrees.

"Don't forget to brush your teeth," I call out down the hall. "You had lots of sugar today," I add as an afterthought as to why she needs to make sure she brushes really good.

"She's either going to crash hard when her head hits the pillow, or she's going to be awake all night with excitement because of Buckley."

"I hope it's the first option. I've got some plans with you, but need her sleeping, first," I tell Lindsay, pulling her in for a quick kiss.

"Is that so, mister?" she asks, walking her fingers up my chest. She smiles up at me, her eyes bright with excitement.

"I've had the need to sink inside you since I first laid eyes on you today. So, the past, oh," I look at the clock and quickly calculate how many hours have gone by since she arrived "eight or so hours have been a small form of torture. My cock has been at half-mast that entire time."

"Mhmm," Lindsay moans quietly. "I could say the same about you."

"Do you think you can stay quiet tonight? Or do I need to turn on the white noise machine?" I watch as a blush creeps up Lindsay's neck and onto her cheeks. The few nights we've spent together this past week when I wasn't working or when Paisley wasn't with me, were not quiet ones. This will be the first night we spend together while I have Paisley.

"I'll do my best, but I can't make any promises, so the

sound machine *might* be a good idea. We don't need to scare the poor girl," she quips.

I nip at her lips, wanting to do more, but I hear the sound of footsteps coming down the hall, so I just press my lips to hers in a chaste kiss and then pull away just as Paisley and Buckley round the corner.

"We're all ready for bed, Daddy," Paisley says. She's in her PJs, and Buckley is sitting next to her like he's ready for bed, as well.

"Alrighty, then, let's get the two of you tucked in and sleeping," I say, pulling away from Lindsay.

"Good night, Paisley, sleep tight," she says to my daughter before we can leave the kitchen.

"Night, Lindsay, thank you for my gift today."

"You're so welcome. I'm glad you had a good birthday party. Thanks for letting me come," she tells her as Paisley walks over and wraps her arms around her in a hug. My own heart beats a little faster, seeing my daughter including Lindsay so easily. She's accepted her into our fold just as quickly as I have, and I couldn't be happier.

11

"Hey, baby, whatcha doing?" Tucker's voice comes across the speakers in my car.

"Just driving, what are you doing?" I ask as I flick my eyes to the rearview mirror before I change lanes on the highway.

"Just woke up. Are you on your way back home?"

"Yep, Allison, and I got everything we went after today. We had fun heading into the city and shopping at stores we don't usually go to," I tell him as I flick my eyes over at Allison. The smirk on her lips tells me she's thinking about the adult store we stopped at on a whim.

"Glad y'all had a good time. How long until you're back in town?" he asks.

"We're about halfway back, so maybe thirty minutes or so, but it will be at least an hour before I can get to your place. I've got to drop Allison off, first, and help her unload all her things."

"Okay, should I plan on you for dinner tonight, or

better yet, how about I take my two favorite girls out tonight?"

"If you want, or we could order in pizza or something easy," I suggest.

"Whatever you want, babe."

"I'm easy. How about you ask Paisley what she'd want? She's the picky one."

"Easy, huh?" he quips, and Allison snickers next to me.

"Tucker!" I exclaim. "You're on speaker. Allison can hear you. Keep it clean."

"I'm not going to say anything she hasn't probably heard out of Lee's mouth." He chuckles.

"Don't be an ass, or you won't be getting any tonight," I tell him sternly.

"Damn, them some fighting words," Allison interjects.

"I'd wear you down," Tucker boasts.

"Don't get too cocky, mister. I could always just go stay at my place tonight," I remind him.

"You could, but then you wouldn't have my arms holding you all night, and you know you want that."

"Yeah, yeah, yeah," I grumble, knowing that he's got me on that point.

"I'll find out from Paisley what she wants for dinner, and we'll see you in an hour or so, drive safe," he says.

"Sounds good; just text me if you call something in and want me to pick it up on my way over," I offer before we disconnect the call.

"So, how is it dating a single dad?" Allison asks.

"It's fine. She's actually a pretty cool kid, and we get along really well."

"How's his co-parenting relationship with her mom?"

"They seem to have a pretty good thing going on. I've only been around her at Paisley's party, and that was fine. She was really nice to me, didn't act like I was stepping on anyone's toes. Tucker told me that they agreed before Paisley was even born to always keep her the priority and to work together to parent her," I tell her.

"That's so rare to hear, but refreshing. I'm glad that they've made it work."

"It really is. I think that maybe because they were never actually together, just a friends with benefits kind of situation, that there wasn't that hurt from a break-up involved. No backstabbing was going on."

"Oh, that's a good point. Shows off his mature side," Allison states.

"I think that it makes him that much sexier. Knowing that he's not one to play games or use his daughter as a pawn. She didn't ask to be born into the situation, so why make her a victim."

"Exactly, and I'm happy for you. You guys seem happy together."

"He makes me happy," I say, a smile pulling at my lips. "I know we kind of tip-toed around our attraction for a long time, and for a while there, I thought nothing would come of it. But I guess that if things are meant to be that they will be."

"If anyone deserves to be happy, it's you, babe," Allison says, reaching over and squeezing my arm.

"Right back at cha, girlfriend," I say, looking over at her quick. "Speaking of being happy, how's Lee treating you?"

"Just fine," she says, the smile on her face telling me everything I need to know. "We're just keeping it casual, right now."

"So, just fuck buddies?" I ask.

"You make it sound so crass." She laughs, but I can hear the slight hurt in her words.

"Why not ask him for more? I can tell that's what you want," I press.

"Because that's not what he wants, right now, and I don't want to ruin what we do have going."

"You deserve more than to be someone's booty call," I tell her.

"I know," she says, her voice cracking. I look over quick and catch her swiping at a tear falling from her lashes. "I thought that I was good with the friends with benefits arrangement, but I don't know that I am, after all," she admits.

"So, tell him. Put it all out there, and he needs to either shit or get off the pot. He can't have his cake and eat it too, in this situation. If friends with benefits isn't working for you, then it can't be an option for him. Don't settle just to make him happy."

"You make it sound so easy," she says, sniffling. I reach into my center console and pull out a few tissues, handing them over.

"The few times I've been around him, lately, he's been very into you. I imagine he's just scared or used to the friends with benefits arrangement. But given a chance to be in an actual committed relationship, he might flourish and be the best boyfriend."

"And if he says it's friends with benefits or nothing?" she asks.

"Then you hold your head up high, tell him good luck with his right hand, and you walk away with your dignity, knowing that you stood up for yourself. It will be his loss, and if that happens, I won't be surprised if he's groveling at your feet within a week, asking for a second chance."

"You're good for my ego." Allison's tears turn to laughs. "I'll take your words under advisement," she says as I pull in to her place.

"Want me to stick around and help you set things up?" I ask before we get out to unload.

"No, I'm going to just relax, bust out a bottle of wine and call it a night. Plus, you've got a sexy man waiting on you. He wouldn't be pleased with me if I kept you longer than I already have."

"He'd get over it," I tell her. "I'm not dropping my friends just because I have a boyfriend. Sisters before misters," I say, flashing her an exaggerated wink.

Allison doubles over, laughing. "He'd be so mopey about it, and you know it," she finally says.

"Maybe," I admit. "But he'd get over it. BJs go a long way in turning a man's attitude around."

"You know it," she agrees with me, her attitude already turning back around.

We unload my car in a few trips, leaving only my things in the back.

"Thanks for going with me today. It was just what we needed." I pull Allison into a hug once we've set everything down inside her place.

"Agreed. Let's plan on a pedicure night sometime soon."

"Of course!" I tell her before I head out. I look back once more before she closes the door behind me, and know that things will be fine for my best friend. She's just got to stand up for herself and show that man how good things could be for them if he'd just give things a shot. Maybe I'll bring things up to Tucker and see what he thinks, since he knows Lee just as well as I know Allison.

I pull out of Allison's place and head for my own. I unload my things in just two trips. I didn't need as much as she did, and my items weren't as large. She needed some new shelves from IKEA, where I just got a few kitchen things and some other decorative knickknacks. I even picked up a couple small things for Tucker's house.

"Hello," I answer, my phone buzzing on the kitchen counter where it rests next to my keys.

"Hey, baby. Are you going to be here soon?" Tucker's voice fills my kitchen.

"Just finished putting things away. Did you ever decide on dinner?"

"Paisley wants pizza. Do you have any issues with that?"

"That sounds good to me. Are we going out or ordering in?" I ask, picking up my phone from the counter and heading toward my bedroom. I pull out my overnight bag, placing it on the end of my bed. I toss in some underwear and a clean bra, along with some pajamas. Since Paisley will be over, I insist on sleeping with clothes on, much to Tucker's arguments.

"I was thinking of taking the two of you to Blaze. That way, we all get exactly what we want."

"Sounds good to me," I tell him, grabbing a pair of jeans and a T-shirt from my closet. "I'm just packing an overnight bag now, so I should be on my way over shortly."

"Or we could just swing by and pick you up," Tucker offers.

"That works just as well," I confirm.

"All right, I'll crate up Buckley and get Paisley loaded, and we'll be over to get you. See you in ten minutes, tops."

"See you then," I confirm before the line goes quiet. I finish grabbing my things and packing them into my bag before I close it up and carry it out and set it by the door. I pop back into the bathroom quick, making sure that I look okay, before heading out to dinner with Tucker and Paisley.

I'm just finishing up when I hear a knock at my door. A smile tugs at my lips as I make my way to the door. I open it up to find Tucker standing there with a dancing Paisley.

"Mind if she uses your bathroom? She informed me when we were almost here that she had to go super bad," Tucker asks as I look down and see the look on Paisley's face.

"Of course, right in there, sweetie." I point toward the hall bathroom, and she takes off running.

"Sorry, she said she didn't need to go when I asked at home," Tucker says, wrapping an arm around my waist and pulling me against him.

"It's not a problem. A girl's got to pee when a girl's got to pee," I remind him just as his lips land on mine. I melt into him, his dominance taking hold as he deepens the kiss. He backs me against the wall, pressing his entire body to mine. I can feel every ridge of muscle and how hard I'm making him. The click of the bathroom door opening breaks his hold, and he pulls back slightly. His lips land on my forehead, leaving a kiss before he takes a small step back.

"Feel better?" he asks his daughter as she comes back over to where we're standing just inside the door.

"Yes! I had to go bad," she tells us.

"Yet, at home, you told me you didn't need to," Tucker reminds her.

"The bumpy road made me have to, Daddy," she tells him, her sass coming out.

"Oh, the bumps, huh?" he asks. I don't really know of that many bumps in the road between our houses, but whatever, she's little and cute, and as I told him, when a girl's got to go, a girl's got to go.

"Who's hungry?" I ask, bringing both of their attention my way.

"Me!" Paisley cheers, jumping up and down.

"Then let's go!" Tucker says. He grabs my overnight bag from the floor, and I grab my keys, check my back pocket for my phone and grab a light jacket from the coat hook on the wall. Paisley bounces her way out my door and toward Tucker's truck, him on her heels while I lock up and then follow, myself.

"How's Buckley today?" I ask Paisley, turning slightly in my seat to look at her in the back.

"He's good! We took him down to the pond, and he went swimming!"

"That sounds fun! Did you throw the ball in for him?" I ask.

"Yep," she replies.

"What else did you do?" I ask as Tucker drives us down the road. His hand slides over and finds mine, our fingers entwining as he rests our connected hands on my thigh.

"Cuddled with him and Daddy while we watched a show, played inside, colored," she tells me, ticking things off on her fingers.

"Sounds like a fun day."

"Yep. What did you do?"

"I went shopping in the big city with my best friend."

"I's love shopping! Did you buy me anything?" she asks, and I can't help but laugh at her question.

"Paisley." Tucker tries to reprimand her for asking.

"I didn't, but I also wasn't really at a place that would sell anything that you might want. I was helping my friend buy some shelves and things for her house."

"Oh," she puffs out, her shoulders falling forward only slightly since she's buckled in with the five-point harness of her car seat.

"Maybe next time I go shopping, I can find something for you," I tell her, and her head pops up, and a smile fills her face.

"Really?" she asks, excited.

"Give me some ideas, and I'll keep them in mind," I tell her.

"You don't have to buy her anything," Tucker murmurs from the driver's seat.

"I know I don't have to, but what if I want to?" I ask him, turning my attention to him.

"I just don't want you thinking that you have to, or for Paisley to think that it is a requirement."

"I promise you that I don't feel obligated, and I won't make it an everyday occurrence. But if I see something that I think she'll like, I'll pick it up. Is that okay with you? I also don't want to step on anyone's toes. You are her parent."

"That's fine. I just don't want her expecting things from people."

"You're a good dad, you know that?"

"I try my best. I have one hell of a role model to follow after," he says as he pulls into the parking lot of the mall. The place we're going tonight is located in one of the spaces that have its own outside entrance. Tucker parks, and we all jump out. Paisley grabs my hand and then her dad's as we cross the distance to the doors.

12

TUCKER

I LOOK ACROSS THE TABLE AT MY GIRLS. PAISLEY INSISTED on sitting next to Lindsay once we'd gone through the line and had our pizzas built and placed in the wood fire oven. Paisley now has pizza sauce covering both of her cheeks from the way she's bitten into slices of her pizza. I wink at Lindsay while we listen to Paisley tell another story about her and Buckley outside today.

Sitting here with these two has me thinking ahead; what it would be like to have this forever, maybe another kid or two filling the booth with us. Seeing how well my daughter has taken to having another woman in my life has me kicking myself for not pursuing things sooner. But I also realize that things happen when they do for a reason.

"What do you say we stop at the cupcake shop in the parking lot before we head home?" I ask Paisley as we box up our leftovers.

"Can I get a unicorn one?" she asks.

"If they have one, sure, why not?" I agree.

We clean off our table, taking the boxes with us to drop in the truck before we walk across the parking lot for the cupcake place. Paisley slides right back between Lindsay and me, holding both of our hands, swinging them back and forth like only a five-year-old can. "Swing me!" she demands between giggles. She hops, pulling her feet up as we swing her between the two of us. The sound of laughter fills my ears as I listen to Lindsay's laughter mixed with Paisley's. Seeing these two together, and having such a great time with one another, just melts my heart that much more. The horror stories I've heard from other single dads on how their kids and girlfriends get along had me always shying away from introducing anyone that I attempted to date since Paisley was born.

"All right, let's get you cleaned up," I tell Paisley, handing over a napkin so that she can wipe her frosting-covered face. She lucked out and got the last unicorn cupcake the shop had. The pink and purple frosting piled high on top now covers her cheeks, nose, and even some on her chin.

"Let me help," Lindsay offers, taking a clean napkin from the holder on the table. She wipes at the frosting, rather than smearing it like Paisley was doing. "Actually, let's go to the bathroom, and we can wash it better in there."

"I can take her," I offer, not wanting Lindsay to feel obligated to take care of Paisley.

"I've got it," she insists, resting her hand on my shoulder. "We'll be right back," she says, squeezing where her hand rests before they head down the little hall to the girls' bathroom.

"Your daughter is super cute," the young woman that helped us and who is now wiping down tables says.

"Thanks. She's the best."

"Daddy, Daddy," Paisley calls out as she bounces down the hall. Maybe the sugar rush from the cupcake wasn't my brightest idea tonight.

"What?" I asked, bouncing my head up and down, matching each of her bouncing steps. She reaches me and finally comes to a stop.

"Lindsay said she'd braid my hair after I take a bath tonight!"

"She did, did she?" I ask, looking up at Lindsay now that she's joined us, and see her nodding her agreement.

"That I did," she confirms. "But only after she has a bath and her hair is washed. She somehow got frosting in it, so I figured that was the best way to get it out. Sorry if a bath wasn't in the plans tonight," she says apologetically.

"We can definitely handle a bath," I say. "How about we get out of here and head home. I think we've got just enough time for a bath, hair braiding time, and then bed," I say to both of them as I bounce Paisley on my knee where she's perched. "Sound good?"

"Sounds like a plan to me," Lindsay agrees, as does Paisley.

I set Paisley down, then stand and grab the used napkins from the table and toss them in the trash before heading back outside. I snag Lindsay's hand, entwining our fingers and giving her hand a little squeeze.

"Daddy, can you carry me?" Paisley asks, not even five feet out the door.

"Sure can," I tell her, swooping her up in my arms.

Once situated, I slip my hand back into Lindsay's as we cross the parking lot for my truck.

———

"WELL, WELL, WELL, WHAT IS GOING ON IN HERE?" I ASK from the doorway. It took me two books before Paisley was asleep tonight. That's after a half-hour bath, followed by Lindsay brushing out and then braiding her hair, all while we watched an episode on Disney Junior.

"I figured we would do some cuddling of our own, in here," Lindsay says, patting the bed next to her. I don't need another invitation. I reach behind me and grab the collar of my T-shirt and tug it over my head, tossing it toward the hamper in the corner. My bedroom door closes behind me with a click. I unfasten my belt, letting it hang open as I pop the top button on my jeans. Since Lindsay is already under the covers and she's got them pulled up completely, I can only assume she's mostly naked underneath.

"Yes, ma'am," I finally reply. I shuck my jeans and socks, leaving me in only a pair of boxer briefs. My cock is already standing at full mast, ready to find the sexy woman underneath the blankets.

I pull back the blankets on my side, leaving Lindsay covered, still. I slide onto the mattress, situating myself on my side, facing her. "Come here," I growl, reaching out and pulling her flush against me. My hands roam up and down her warm, naked flesh until I come to a bra and lower until I feel her panties. I can work with this.

"Fuck, I've wanted you all damn day," I say before I

suck on the side of her throat. I slip a finger beneath her panties and find her wet. I groan against her skin as I suck a little harder, moving my lips to a new spot as to not leave a hickey on her throat. I don't think she'd be too happy about that come tomorrow.

I break away. "I need these off, now," I instruct, tugging at the waistband of her panties.

"Oh," she says, I think, a little shocked I'm jumping right in. She shimmies out of them and I shuck my own briefs. I grab my cock, squeezing the base to try and calm the blood flow down slightly. I've got plans for tonight, and he's just going to have to wait his turn. I've got a pussy to make come, first, multiple times, if I'm lucky.

"That's better," I say against her lips before I cover them with my own. I take advantage of her opening up for me, our tongues dueling as I kiss her as deeply as I possibly can. The fire that is coursing through my body has me ready to burst. While I kiss the fuck out of her, I tweak her nipples between my fingers now that they're exposed to me. She lost the bra when the panties came off, leaving the two of us naked.

I kiss my way down her body, nipping and sucking her sensitive and most responsive areas. Places like the underside of her breasts, the area just above each hip bone, below her navel, but above her mound. I slide further down the bed, settling my shoulders between her thighs. The smell of her arousal fills my nostrils as I slide the tip of my tongue through her slit.

"Yes!" Lindsay cries at the movement.

"You like that?" I ask, more a rhetorical question. One that I really don't need a verbal answer for. I slide my tongue up and down a few more times, purposely avoiding her clit with each pass. I know that's the one spot she really wants my mouth, but I want her coming apart at the seams before I give in. Building up the anticipation, I slide a finger inside her, immediately feeling her muscles clench around it I find that bundle of nerves on the inside and rub it softly.

A string full of jibberish falls from Lindsay's lips as I continue my assault, looking for the few seconds of pure bliss. I finally take pity, flicking my tongue over the bundle of nerves that makes up her clit. I suck it hard into my mouth and increase the thrusts of my fingers. Because of the amount of time I spent building her up, she exploded on my fingers and tongue in a matter of seconds. I slow my strokes, sliding my fingers from her pussy. I kiss her inner thighs, first, then drop a few more open-mouthed kisses to her skin as I push up the bed. Once back up near the pillows, I reach over and grab a condom from the nightstand. I tear the package open with my teeth, then roll it down my cock. I stroke myself a few times while I wait for Lindsay to come down from her intense orgasm.

"Are you ready?" I ask.

"Yes," Lindsay agrees. I tug her until she's straddling me. I can feel my cock sliding through her folds as she moves her hips back and forth over the top of me.

"I need inside you, baby," I tell her as I reach between us and line my cock up with her entrance. She starts to sink down, her body pulsing around the crown. I hold on to her hips and thrust up hard until I can't fill her any more. "Fuck, you're tight," I grit out, grinding my molars to keep from being loud. The last thing we need right now is Paisley busting through the door.

"Ride me," I instruct once Lindsay adjusts to me being inside of her. She rotates her hips a few times, finding what is going to work best. Her hands pressed against my chest, and my hands still on her hips as I help guide her body up and down as she bounces on my shaft. Her body is squeezing me as she builds towards her release.

"I'm close," she moans out, her movements becoming a little more ragged as she chases her release.

"That's it, babe. Come on my cock," I tell her, sliding a hand between us and finding her clit with my thumb. I press against the bundle of nerves, rubbing it just how I know she likes it. I feel her orgasm hit; her bouncing stops as she collapses forward, her mouth resting next to my ear as she pants heavily through the release. I grip her hips once more, holding her tight as I thrust up, pounding into her as I chase my own release. The tight-ness that envelopes my cock makes the friction on my shaft intensify the sensations. My orgasm barrels down my spine, and I pull her lips to my own to keep from yelling out as I come, filling the condom.

I break the kiss, gulping in air as I work to catch my breath. "You good?" I ask, running my hand up and down Lindsay's back. She's lying on top of me, my cock still buried deep inside her warm body.

"Perfect," she murmurs, her breath hitting my neck.

I lay there for a few minutes, completely content to bask in the hormones. The only noise is that of our labored breathing as we both work on slowing down. The moment is broken when Lindsay pushes up until she is sitting, still straddling me with my softening cock inside of her. I purposely twitch it, causing the most beautiful laugh to fall from her lips.

"How about a shower before we fall asleep?" I suggest.

"Yes," she says, sliding off me. I immediately miss her warmth and tightness.

I follow her to the bathroom, stopping to grab two clean towels from the cabinet. She turns on the water while I dispose of the condom. I watch as she rummages through her bathroom bag that sits on my counter, pulling something out. I watch as she pulls her hair up and into a messy bun on the top of her head before she steps into the shower.

I follow her, taking a few seconds to adjust the warmth of the water. She likes hers a little hotter than I like my showers, usually, but it's amazing what I'll put up with for this woman. "Do I get to soap you up?" I ask, wrapping my arms around her body, my hands cupping her breasts as my lips find her exposed neck. With her hair out of the way, it is all open territory for me. I tweak her nipples between my fingers, her ass starts to rub against my cock, springing it back to life as I harden against her backside.

"How do you do this to me?" she asks, turning in my arms, hers going around my neck as she presses our bodies flush together. "I already need you again," she tells me before pulling my mouth to hers.

I take control, backing her up against the tile wall. I slide my hands under her ass, lifting her up until her legs wrap around my waist. Pinned against the wall, I devour her mouth as I glide my cock through her folds, hitting her clit with each thrust.

"I need you inside me," she moans.

"I don't have a condom in here," I tell her, needing to remember to stash some in here for future showers.

"I'm on birth control," she says, and I'm caught off guard. Is she saying what I think she is? "And I'm clean."

"What are you saying, Lindsay?" I question, needing to know what she is alluding to. I need to know that she's okay with me going bare inside of her. I've never done that, to my knowledge. Lilly and I are confident that a failed condom is what got us Paisley.

"I'm okay with it if you are. If you aren't, then that's okay," she rambles.

"I'm more than okay with it, baby." I kiss her hard, wanting her to know that I'm more than okay with this.

"I've never," I remind her. "And, of course, I'm clean, but are you sure? I don't want any regrets to come tomorrow morning," I tell her honestly.

"Tucker, if you don't fuck me right now, I'm going to leave this shower and go take care of things myself."

"Yes, ma'am," I reply, even if the idea of watching her pleasure herself doesn't make my cock ache and leak with a few drops of pre-cum. I reach down, grabbing my cock; I slide the tip through her folds one more time before lining us up. I thrust my hips up, filling her completely. The feeling of her bare has my eyes crossing. The way her body envelopes me has me thinking this is what heaven must be like.

I find a fast rhythm, bottoming out with each thrust.

The wall helps pin Lindsay's body exactly where I need her to be. My lips find their way back to hers, and I kiss her deeply as I piston my hips, filling her with fast and deep thrusts. I swallow her cries as she comes all over my cock. The way her body convulses around my cock has as my own orgasm racing through my body. I snap my hips one last time against her and feel as my body unleashes and fills her with my cum. My mind jumps forward to visions of her belly swollen with our child, and it does nothing but spur on my desire for this woman.

13

LINDSAY

"WE'VE GOT TWO MVAs INBOUND. ADULT WOMAN AND A female minor!" Betty calls out after she hangs up with one of the inbound ambulance crews.

"I'm on it," I call out, jumping up from my chair as I pull out a gown and face shield to get on so I'm fully protected when the ambulance arrives, and the patient is in front of us.

Dr. Knight comes up beside me as we wait at the ambulance doors; I can hear the sirens as they pull into the bay, and wait for them to come to a stop before the back door pops open and the paramedic jumps out. Allison and Dr. Murray go to meet that patient, and Dr. Knight and I take the second one that pulls in just a few seconds later.

The paramedic who was driving the second ambulance starts calling out information to us before he reaches the back door. "Female passenger, five years old. Was properly secured in a five-point harness. She's got a fractured arm and is complaining of belly, chest, and neck pain," he says, and I take in everything he's just told me. The doors finally pop open, and the stretcher is pulled out. It isn't until the stretcher is next to me that I realize that the little girl in front of me is Paisley. The scared look on her face makes tears spring to my eyes. I suck in a deep breath, willing my tears to go away. I've got to be strong for her in this moment.

"Lindsay!" she cries. "Where's my mommy?"

"I'm right here, baby. Your mommy is being looked at by another doctor; she's in the next room over," I tell her, pointing in the direction of the other trauma bay.

"I want my mommy and daddy," Paisley calls out again.

"I know, baby, and I'll have someone call Daddy, okay?"

"Okay," she sniffles as everyone gets to work on her. Dr. Knight assesses her, calling out orders to everyone. I work on keeping her calm as I administer some pain meds he's ordered. We draw labs, x-rays are taken to confirm the broken arm, as well as to check for other fractures. Thankfully, the exam and ultrasound show no internal bleeding, so no need for surgery.

"Where's my daughter?" I hear an all too familiar deep voice from the hall. "She was brought in by an ambulance, car accident. I need to see my daughter!" he booms again.

"Sir, calm down. I'll see what I can find out for you," one of the new interns says to Tucker. I step out of Paisley's treatment room and close the distance to him.

"I've got this," I say to the intern at the desk. "Tucker," I get his attention.

"Lindsay," his voice cracks, and he brings his fist up to his mouth, biting back another outburst. "Please tell me she's okay. She has to be okay."

"She's going to be just fine. Nothing a pink cast won't fix in just a few weeks," I tell him. "Now, take a deep breath, and you can go in and see her."

He wraps his arms around me, burying his face in my neck, and I can feel his body shaking as he sobs. I can't imagine the call he got, informing him his daughter was at the ER after being in an accident.

I hold him close, shouldering his pain as he lets it all out. He's got his turnout pants on since he's on shift right now, and if he leaves the firehouse, not only is his entire truck probably here, but they have to be ready to go if they were to be called out.

"Ready to go see your girl?" I ask once he's pulled himself back together.

"Yes, please take me to her." I grip his hand and lead him into the trauma bay.

"Paisley," he sighs her name as he steps through the door. He assesses her as she lays on the bed. We've splinted her arm, as we're still waiting on ortho to come for her consult to determine if she needs surgery, or if we can just cast it.

"Daddy," her tired voice calls out as tears slide down her cheeks.

"I'm here, sweetheart," he tells her, moving to her side. He wipes at her face with his fingers. She looks so small compared to him, but he's so gentle. I'm sure being a little more so right now than he would if he was wiping away tears from a fall or some other reason she might cry.

"Where's Mommy?" she asks again.

"The doctors are still fixing her up," I tell her. "They should be done soon, and then maybe we can take you to see her, or she can come to see you."

"Mr. Wild," Dr. Knight states as he steps back into the trauma bay. He goes over everything that he's found out so far from test results and what we're still waiting on, and why we might even need that information. "Overall, Paisley is fortunate; she was protected so well in her car seat. I'm confident that you'll be taking her home sometime today with just a cast and some pain meds for the next few days. Once we get that ortho consult, we'll know for sure how to proceed," he finishes telling Trucker.

"You're sure no head injuries or internal problems?" Tucker questions.

"I'm confident she's got neither of those. Her belly was tender upon our first assessment of her, but the ultrasound we performed didn't show any evidence of her bleeding internally. The tenderness is consistent with where her straps were, so I'm confident that it's just from the impact of the accident. But, we'll for sure keep an eye on her while she's here and make sure no changes are noted."

"Thanks, Doc. And her mother, she's okay?" Tucker asks.

"I'm not the doctor on her case, but I'll see what we can find out. Are you family?" he asks.

"Only because we have a daughter together," Tucker tells him.

"Then, we'll have to get permission from the patient

or her family before we can relay any information to you; I'm sorry," he tells Tucker.

"I understand." Tucker sinks down into the chair next to Paisley's bed, his hand holding on to hers as he rests his forehead against the side of the mattress.

"I'll go check-in and find out if we can update you," I tell Tucker before I duck out. I walk over and peek into the bay that Lilly is in and see the doctors and nurses still attending to her. She looks pretty beat up, but she isn't intubated, so I take that as a good sign.

"Excuse me, are you Lindsay?" a man standing to the side and out of the way asks. I recognize him from Paisley's party as her stepdad.

"I am," I confirm. I don't really expect him to remember me, especially in a situation like this.

"Where's Paisley? Is she okay?" he asks.

"She's in the next bay over; Tucker is in with her. Would you like to see her?" I ask, keeping my voice calm to try and help keep him calm.

"Yes, I know that Lilly would like an update on her."

"Follow me; Paisley was also asking about her mom, so you can update her. I was actually coming to ask if it was okay if I updated her since Tucker was with her. We can't release information to him about Lilly without her or your approval."

"That's fine," Mike says, running his hand through his hair. It's all messed up, like he's done that multiple times today already.

"Paisley." Mike says her name as he steps inside her room. Her eyes fly open as she takes him in.

"Where's Mommy?" she asks him.

"She's still with the doctors, but she's going to be okay. She just has a few minor cuts and bruises and a broken leg."

"I's have a broken arm. Can we have matching casts?" Paisley asks Tucker and Mike.

"I'll see what requests I can put in for matching casts," I pipe in, signing into the computer to check on the status of her ortho consult.

"Lilly's going to be okay, then?" Tucker asks Mike, stretching his hand across the bed to shake Mike's hand.

"Yes, they're cleaning out some glass right now from her head, and I think waiting to hear from ortho on her leg, but otherwise she's going to be fine, albeit sore for a week or so. She's been asking about Paisley, so let me go update her, and then I'll check back."

"We'll be here," Tucker tells him as he ducks out.

"Ortho should be here any minute now. They've noted in the computer that her x-rays have been reviewed, and the next step is to come down and relay their recommendations to the patient and you," I tell Tucker as I sign out of the computer.

"Thank you," he says, looking at his daughter and then back to me. "This situation is my worst fear, something happening to her and me not being there to be with her. Thank you for taking care of her when I couldn't."

"She was a trooper, and I'd have done everything I did for her for any of my patients."

"Yeah, but knowing that she wasn't alone in a room full of strangers, scared and in pain, makes me feel a little better. Getting that call at the station made my heart fall into my stomach. The drive over here felt like it took years, not minutes."

"Is the entire truck here?" I ask, realizing that Tucker hasn't left Paisley's side since he got here.

"I'm sure they are. Dad called in to dispatch and took us out of service, for now. We won't usually leave someone behind in a situation like this. We're family. Where I go, they go, and vice versa."

"Would you like me to update them on Paisley?"

"Can you?"

"I can, with your permission, of course."

"That'd be great. I'll send a text to my parents updating them. I'm sure they're out in the waiting room by now."

"I'll go see who I can find. I'll be right back," I tell him. I hesitate slightly before leaving the room, and walk around the bed to where he's sitting. I drop a kiss to his cheek, doing my best to give him my strength. "She's going to be just fine," I whisper against his cheek.

He turns his head, planting his lips against mine in a chaste kiss. There's nothing sexual behind it, just pure emotions. "Thanks," he says again, wrapping one arm around me while his other stays, holding Paisley's hand. He hugs me as tightly as he can with one arm for a few seconds, finally letting me go so I can go update everyone from the firehouse waiting to hear how she's doing.

14

TUCKER

I SIT NEXT TO MY DAUGHTER'S HOSPITAL BED, MY HEAD resting against the mattress while the beeping of the monitors fills the room. She's sleeping, the pain meds doing their job of relaxing her and taking the pain away. When Dad walked into the TV room at the firehouse looking white as a ghost, he told me to get my ass to the hospital. He'd hardly gotten the words out of his mouth, and I was on my feet, along with everyone else on my truck, and out the doors. I don't recall much of the drive over, except feeling like it was taking forever to get the few miles down the road. I know Dad followed behind us, taking care of calling Mom to fill her in on what little information he had at the time.

I don't know what I would have done if it was our truck that had responded to the accident. I'd have probably lost my shit right there at the scene. Knowing that it was another firehouse that responded tells me that the accident happened outside of our response zone, which

143

isn't that big of a surprise since Lilly lives in a different district than I work. Hell, even I live in another district.

"Mr. Wild." An older, deep voice pulls me from my racing thoughts. I look up, then stand and accept the hand that is stretched across the bed for me.

"Tucker, nice to meet you."

"Tucker, I'm Dr. Mills from Orthopedics. I've had the chance to look over Paisley's x-rays and am here to inform you that she'll be just fine. A cast for the next six weeks, and she should be back to normal. No damage to her growth plates and no need for surgery. We'll get the bones set properly and get her all casted up and on her way home."

I blow out a huge breath; the weight of knowing Paisley is okay and only needs a cast and not surgery is lifted from my chest. "Thank you so much. Will that happen here, or will we need to bring her into your office for that?" I ask.

"We'll get her casted here. I don't want to risk any further damage to the arm. I'll see her in my office in six weeks, sooner if her pain in the arm isn't subsiding after the next few days."

"We can handle that. She asked if it would be possible to have a matching cast with her mom, who's in the next room over," I tell him.

"I'll see what we can do," he muses, jotting some notes down on the tablet he carries.

"Is that your wife next door?" he asks, looking at the tablet again.

"Um, no. Just Paisley's mom. We co-parent. I believe

her husband, Mike, is in with her," I tell him, trying hard to not feel judged by this man.

"Right, I'll go check on her next and see what we can do about matching casts, if they both need them," he tells me without really telling me anything. I don't expect them to give me all of Lilly's information. I'm fully aware of how medical privacy laws work. Being a first responder, we're taught to give as little information to those around us as possible, as we don't know who is privy to that or not.

"Mommy!" Paisley calls out as the door opens wider, and a wheelchair rolls in.

"Paisley." Lilly calls out her name as tears roll down her cheeks. Lilly has a leg propped up, surrounded by pillows and a splint to keep it where they want it. "How are you?" she asks our daughter.

"I'm fine, Mommy. My arm hurts a little," she tells her, holding up her own splinted extremity. "Do we get to have matching casts?" Paisley asks her.

"I think we do," Lilly tells her, Mike rolling her as close to Paisley's bed as he can. I hop up and move some things out of the way so he can get her right next to the bed, close enough that they can touch one another.

"Can we get purple?" Paisley asks, a hint of excitement in her voice.

"If they have it, I don't see why not," Lilly answers her.

"How are you doing?" I finally interrupt, asking Lilly.

"Sore, tired, and feel like I've been hit by a truck," she tells me, a little humor lacing her tired words.

"What happened?" I ask. I know they were in an accident, but I don't know any of the specifics.

"A truck ran a red light and T-boned me, sent me spinning around, and caused me to hit the car next to us. My car is a complete loss."

"That's okay, sweetheart, we can get you a new one," Mike chimes in, resting a supportive hand on Lilly's shoulder as he leans down and drops a kiss to the top of her head.

"I know, I just keep thinking what-ifs. What if Owen had been in the car? The truck hit me right at his door. Would he have been hurt badly? It's bad enough that Paisley and I were hurt." She starts to cry, and Mike comforts her as best as he can with her in the wheelchair.

I realize I didn't even think about their baby and whether he was in the car or hurt. "Where is Owen?" I ask.

"He's with my parents," Mike answers. "He was with them while Lilly and Paisley had an afternoon together," he explains.

I nod, accepting his explanation. "The only thing that matters is that both of you are okay and will heal up completely in just a few weeks."

"Knock-knock." A younger girl raps her knuckles on the doorjamb before she pulls the curtain open further so she can get in the doorway, along with her cart.

"I hear someone pretty special in here needs a cast." She smiles at Paisley as she places her cart at the end of the bed and starts pulling out some supplies.

"Can it be purple?" Paisley perks up and asks.

"Sure, can! Do you want light or dark purple? I have both," she tells her, pulling out a roll of both cast colors.

"The dark one!" Paisley exclaims.

"Or I can use both and give you a pattern," the aide offers.

I can tell the wheels inside Paisley's mind are turning as she mulls over the decision. She looks between Lilly and me, looking to see if we're going to interject and make the decision for her.

"Just the dark purple, please," she finally decides.

"Sounds good. Now, I'm Jasmine, sorry if I didn't introduce myself already," she apologizes, looking between all the adults in the room.

"No worries," Lilly answers for all of us.

"I'll be casting your arm for you. Can you tell me your name, first?"

"Paisley Grace Wild," she states proudly.

"Perfect, and how old are you, Paisley?" Jasmine asks as she looks at her tablet.

"I'm five," Paisley tells her.

"Looks like you just had a birthday not too long ago," Jasmine says as she places the items she'll need to cast the arm on the bed.

"Yep! It was fun!" Paisley answers.

"Did you get anything special?" she asks.

"Daddy got me a dog! Buckley is my favorite."

"Wow, you must be pretty special. I bet Buckley will take good care of you while you recover from breaking your arm," Jasmine tells her.

"Maybe. He likes to cuddle with me," Paisley answers.

"I'm sorry to ask this, but can you move so I can get her casted?" Jasmine asks me.

"Of course," I tell her, standing up from my seat. I kiss the top of Paisley's head before stepping away so that Jasmine can get in and cast her arm. With Lilly positioned on the other side of the bed but not able to move easily because of the wheelchair and her own splinted leg, it was just easiest for me to move out of the way.

I move to the doorway, leaning against the jamb as I watch Jasmine go to work on casting Paisley's arm.

"Mommy's going to get a matching cast," Paisley tells Jasmine as she finishes up.

"That will be cool. You'll have to sign each other's casts and make sure to take lots of pictures together."

"We can sign them?" Paisley asks, almost in awe of the possibilities of having it signed.

"Of course. That's one of the fun parts of having a cast, getting all your friends and family members to sign it."

"That's so cool," Paisley says. "Look, Daddy! Isn't my cast so awesome?" she asks me excitedly.

"It is! Just be careful with that, now. You can hurt someone if you hit them with it."

"Okay. Can I go home now?" Paisley asks as Jasmine cleans up the scraps and trash from casting her arm.

"Soon, baby," I tell her. "I'll go see if I can find out when they'll be ready to discharge you."

I step out of the room and head to the nurses' station. I stand by while Lindsay talks to one of the doctors, relaying information back and forth about a patient.

"How's Paisley doing?" Lindsay asks, coming over to stand in front of me.

"They just finished casting her," I tell her, itching to touch her but knowing that this isn't the time or place. "Do you know when she might be released now that she's been casted?"

"I'll check with Dr. Knight, but it shouldn't be too much longer," Lindsay tells me, all business-like. "Oh, and I updated the guys and your parents. They're all in the waiting room."

"Thanks," I tell her, running a hand over my face. The exhaustion that hits me now that the adrenaline has worn off from being called in from the station because of Paisley's accident, has me ready for a long hot shower and a bed. One preferably filled with the beauty standing in front of me.

"Is she going home with you or Lilly?" Lindsay asks.

"I figured I'd take her home since Lilly is going to need extra help, and Mike will have his hands full between her and the baby. I can take a few days off work to stay home with Paisley while she recovers."

"Okay, I'll get everything ready and let you know when you can spring her free from here," Lindsay tells me before she has to head off into another patient's room. I decide a quick detour out to the waiting room will help me pass the time, plus, I need someone to head back to the station and bring me my truck.

"How is she?" Mom asks, seeing me first as I push through the doors that separate the waiting room from the actual emergency room.

"She's going to be just fine. They just finished casting

her arm. Hopefully, we'll be sprung from here soon," I tell everyone at once.

"Hey," I turn to Lee, "I need a favor; I need my truck. Can you go get it for me?" I ask him, reaching for my pocket, I realize my keys are still back at the station in my locker and tell him as much.

"Of course, anything else, man?" he asks.

"Not that I can think of at the moment." He swirls his finger in the air in a circular motion, signaling rounding up everyone.

"Let's go, boys," he tells our truck crew. They all file past me, smacking my back in their support as they head outside so they can return to the firehouse for the rest of our shift.

I turn to my parents, the only two people left from the large group that was here for my daughter and me. "Let this be my notice. I need a few days off. I'm planning on bringing Paisley home with me for now, so I'll need to be home with her," I tell my dad. It's kind of nice to have Dad as my boss in situations like this. He'd probably kick me out of the firehouse if I tried to come back to work this week.

"Of course, I've already called in someone to fill your spot for the next few shifts. You focus on that little girl back there; she's priority number one," Dad tells me.

"How's Lilly?" Mom asks.

"Banged up a little, had some glass in her skull, and she's got a broken leg. Paisley asked for matching casts, so that should be happening," I tell her.

"How fun for them, gotta find the good in the situation," Mom states.

"I guess so. I never want to see her like that again," I tell my mom, honestly. "When Dad came into the room, he hadn't even said a word yet, and I knew something was wrong. Just the look on his face and his coloring told me something was going on."

"I understand, son, I was just as shocked when he called me and told me to be ready for him to pick me up on his way to the hospital."

"I'll call you once I've got her home and settled. Maybe you can come over and see her tonight. I'm sure she'd love to have visitors," I tell Mom, pulling her into a much-needed hug.

"I'd like that very much," she says, her words slightly muffled as she talks into my chest.

"Call if you need anything," Dad instructs. I stand and watch as he leads my mom out the door and into the parking lot. It won't surprise me if he drops her off at home, and she starts whipping up Paisley's favorite foods to bring over to my place, so we have them on hand.

I head back to her treatment room, finding that Lilly and Mike have left, and she's talking to Lindsay.

"Hey, how's it going in here?" I ask, smiling at my girls. I love thinking of these two as mine.

"Someone is ready to be sprung free," Lindsay says, flashing me a smile.

"Lee should be here shortly with my truck, so once he texts me that he's back, I can sign her out."

"Sounds good. I'll just need your signature on a few pages." Lindsay goes over all the discharge paperwork with me, explaining when Paisley will need to follow up with the Orthopedic as well as things to watch for over the next few days and weeks while she heals up.

"Do you mind staying in here with her for a few minutes while I go talk to Lilly and Mike?"

"Of course not," Lindsay assures me. I squeeze her hand quickly before going to talk to Lilly. "Hey, just wanted to let you know that Paisley's been discharged. I was going to take her home, get her settled, and keep her for the next few days. I figured that would help you guys out; Mike will have his hands full taking care of you and the baby."

"Thanks, Tucker. Can you have her come in here before you leave so I can give her a hug and kiss and show her our matching casts?"

"Sure can. Are they going to let you head home anytime soon?"

"I think so, just waiting on the doctor to come in again, I believe."

"Good, I'm sure both of you will do much better at home. Don't worry about P; I've got her covered for however long it takes. I've taken the rest of the week off already, and if you still need help with her next week, Mom is more than willing to help. That goes for anything. If you need help during the day with Owen, and Mike needs to go to work, just call her; she'll be more than willing to pop over, I'm sure of it."

"Thanks, Tucker. We really appreciate it," Lilly says again.

"Let me go get our girl, and I'll be right back." I do just that, bringing Paisley in to say goodbye to her mom, then stop at the nurses' station to say goodbye to Lindsay before I take her out to Lee and my waiting truck.

"Nona wants to know what kind of ice cream or popsicles you want her to bring you," I tell Paisley once I've got her home and settled on the couch. I insisted on carrying her inside the house. Even though I know she's perfectly fine walking on her own, I still don't want anything else happening to her. The pain meds they gave her at the hospital made her a little woozy and sleepy. The last thing I need is her falling while trying to walk because of the side effects of the meds.

"Strawberry," she says as Buckley hops up on the couch next to her, settling into her side. He licks at her fingers that stick out of the cast on her left hand.

"Anything else you want to request before Nona stops at the store on her way over?" I ask, kissing her forehead.

"No, I'm just tired," she tells me.

"Okay, sweetheart. How about you watch some princesses and maybe take a nap, then."

"All right, Daddy," she agrees, shifting until she's comfortable on the couch. Her eyes hardly open as I flip the TV to her favorite channel. I don't expect her to even last this full half-hour episode with how heavy her eyes are.

15

LINDSAY

"HOW'RE THINGS GOING?" I ASK TUCKER AS I APPROACH the porch. He's rocking back and forth on one of the chairs he keeps out here.

"She's been sleeping for a while. I think the pain meds are still in her system," he tells me, holding out a hand for me to take. I do so immediately, and he pulls me onto his lap. I accept the seat, leaning against him and resting my head on his shoulder.

"God, today was terrifying. It feels like an entire week has gone by, and here it is, only seven," he murmurs after a few minutes of silence.

"Traumatic events can do that to you."

"All I want to do is have some dinner and take you to bed. I need to hold you, and I need to sleep," he says, pressing a kiss to the crown of my head.

"Well, you're in luck, because I can make both of those things happen."

"Mom brought over some food, a pan of lasagna and some fresh garlic bread, if that sounds okay to you?"

"That sounds perfect," I assure him. "Do we need to bake it?" I ask. My stomach is already growling in hunger, so I'm hoping that we just need to heat it up.

"Nope, she already cooked it. Wanted it ready and easy for me to heat up."

"Perfect, then I'll go make us up two plates, and we can eat out here, if you want," I offer.

"You don't have to do that; I can help," he offers.

"I know you can, but let me do this," I say, kissing his cheek.

"Okay." He concedes quickly, the exhaustion he's feeling evident.

I hop off his lap and head inside. I find the pan of lasagna in the fridge and portion us out two servings. After both heat up in the microwave, I carry them outside, handing one plate over to Tucker. I settle in on the second rocking chair, and we both dig in to our dinner.

"Has she eaten anything since being home?" I ask once we've both finished our dinner.

"A little peanut butter toast when she had her pain medicine, and a popsicle."

"Good, sometimes the pain meds can make kids' stomachs pretty upset, so making sure she eats when she takes it is important."

"I'll keep that in mind. Hopefully, she won't need the prescribed medication for more than a day or so. I'd rather her take over the counter strength than the narcotics they gave her. I know they are needed for a day or two, but I hope that's long enough."

"I'm sure she'll be back to her normal self quickly.

Kids are pretty resilient and bounce back a lot quicker than we do."

"I hope so. You ready to head inside?" he asks.

"Yep, let me grab our dishes, first."

"I can help," he insists, standing up and grabbing both of our plates. I follow him inside, and while he washes up from dinner, I check on Paisley. She stirs on the couch, her eyes slowly opening up as she comes to.

"Hey, munchkin, how are you feeling?" I ask, holding up and offering the water bottle someone stashed next to her.

She takes the water, sucking down a few mouthfuls before finding her voice and answering me. "Hungry," her little voice squeaks out.

"What would you like to eat?" I ask.

"Maybe a PB and J," she says, snuggling in deeper with her blanket. Buckley jumps down off the couch and heads for the door, obviously needing outside for a bit. Tucker opens the back door for him and steps out on the back deck to watch him while he does his business. A few minutes later, Tucker comes in, just as I'm putting the finishing touches on Paisley's sandwich, slicing it into two large triangles.

"Thanks for taking care of this for me," he says from behind me as he cages me in against the counter. His lips find my exposed neck and shoulder. As they slide along my skin, a shiver runs down my spine, and I can't help the shudder that runs through my body. "Cold?" Tucker chuckles, his lips still pressed against my skin.

"Nope," I tell him, popping the P as I press my ass against his hardening cock, and he groans.

"You're going to pay for that later."

"Promise?" I ask, spinning in his arms. He boxes me in closer and brings his lips to mine.

"Oh, I promise." He grins before stepping back. He grabs the plate I'd placed Paisley's PB and J on, along with a banana and cup of milk, and turns for the living room. He doesn't usually let her eat out there, but today's events are a good reason to break the rules.

"DID YOU GET HER OFF TO BED, OKAY?" I ASK TUCKER AS HE enters the bedroom. I set my kindle down. I was thoroughly engrossed in J. Nathan's newest book.

"Yep, took her meds like a champ. I got her changed into some pajamas and all set up in bed. One book and she was out," he tells me as he pulls off his T-shirt. He'd lost his uniform before I got here, having replaced it with jeans and a well-worn firehouse T-shirt. I don't hide the fact that I'm ogling his sinewy form. All those muscles are popping as he moves, making my mouth water and core clench just thinking about what he can do to my body.

"Might want to wipe that drool up before it hits the bed," Tucker quips, catching my ogling.

"Asshole," I mutter, yet, not really meaning the jab. I swipe a hand along my lip to make sure I'm not actually drooling, and I'm not.

"What was that?" Tucker asks, boxing me in against the bed as he hovers a few inches from my face, a smirk tugging at his lips.

"Don't be a jerk," I say, smacking his chest as I lose control and start giggling.

"Me? A jerk? Never." He gasps and tickles my sides.

"St-stop." I full-on laugh as he finds a very ticklish spot on my side.

"I'm going to go take a quick shower, and then I'll be back to make good on my earlier promise," Tucker says, dropping a kiss to my lips. I slide a hand into his hair at the base of his neck, holding him against me. His tongue slips inside my mouth as he deepens the kiss. I nip at his bottom lip when he pulls back slightly. "Naughty girl, I love it." He smirks against my lips, and I do it again.

"Just keeping you on your toes," I tell him as he pushes back, my hand falling to the bed as he heads for the shower.

I fall back into my book while I wait for him to shower and come to bed, which takes less than five minutes; damn guys and their ability to take a speed shower.

"Miss me?" he asks, sliding into bed and aligning our bodies so we're facing one another. I save my place and tuck my kindle under my pillow.

"Always," I tell him, kissing his cheek. "Hmmm... you smell good."

"Just for you, baby." He slides a hand up my bare thigh, finding me in only panties and a sleep tank. "If I'd have known you were already down to just these," he says, snapping the elastic of my panties, "I don't know that I would have made it into the shower."

"Can't have a dirty boy coming to bed," I tease him.

"Who you calling boy? I'm all man, sweetheart."

"Are you now?" I grin as he plants a kiss on my lips. He tugs me closer, closing the few-inch gap that was previously between us. I can feel every ridge of his abs against my softness. My body is already so ready for him. Knowing precisely what he does to me, my insides are already trembling, ready for the release he's sure to bring.

16

TUCKER

I OPEN MY FRONT DOOR, TIRED FROM A LONG-ASS SHIFT. I'M ready for a shower, beer, food, and bed, and not necessarily in that order.

"Hey," one of my favorite voices calls out from the living room. "How was your shift?" Lindsay asks.

"Humph." It is my only answer.

"Okayyy..." she says, dragging out the word. "That good, huh?" she asks, standing and coming over to give me a hug and a kiss.

"It was long, and we had a really weird-ass call. I'll tell you about it later," I tell her, squeezing my eyes shut as I slide a hand along my forehead and into my hair. I can't unsee the images that are now burned into my head from that call.

"I'm intrigued," she says, pushing up on her toes to kiss me. I slide my hands up her curves until I can cup her cheeks in my palms. My fingers slide back and into her hair; the brown locks feel like silk between my fingers. I deepen the kiss, Lindsay opening up for me without a second thought.

"Daddy," Paisley's voice calls from the other side of the couch, and pulls me from devouring Lindsay right here by the front door.

"Yes, baby?" I call out, my forehead resting against Lindsay's as I calm my breathing and heart rate.

"I'm hungry!" she proclaims.

"Well, then, maybe Daddy should fire up the grill and get some supper made; how does that sound?"

"I want a hot dog!" she calls out.

"That I can do," I call back to Paisley. "And what would you like?" I ask Lindsay.

"I made us some foil packets with potatoes, veggies, and shrimp. They've been marinating for the last few hours."

"Damn, woman, you know your way to a man's heart." The words slip out, and my breath catches. It's way too fucking soon for me to be proclaiming my love for this woman, but I feel it in my bones. It isn't like we haven't known each other our entire lives, but this—whatever this is between us—is still new.

"Gotta keep you on your toes somehow." She winks.

"I'm going to go change quick, and then I'll fire up the grill. Please tell me I have hot dogs in the fridge?"

"You do, a brand new package. Paisley and I stopped at the store after I picked her up this afternoon."

"Thank you." I drop a quick kiss to her lips before I head for my bedroom so I can change.

I was shocked when Lindsay asked if she could pick

Paisley up for me this afternoon so that she'd already be here when I got off. Since she was free for the day and didn't have much going on, she wanted to hang out with her. Something about some baking or something girly she wanted to do with her: I just love the fact that Paisley loves her as much as I do, and that Lindsay reciprocates.

"So, what did you girls get into this afternoon?" I ask Paisley as she sits on one of the deck chairs as I grill dinner.

"It's a surprise, Daddy," she tells me, rolling her eyes. *Damn sassy attitude.*

"You sure you can't tell me?" I prod, trying to get her to crack.

"Nope," she states matter of factly.

"Okay." I exaggerate the word, making Paisley fall into a fit of giggles. "I love you, baby girl."

"I love you, too, Daddy."

"Since you won't tell me what you did with Lindsay, can you at least tell me if you had fun?"

"Yes! She's the best!"

"It makes me happy that the two of you get along so well," I tell my daughter, knowing that she doesn't get the meaning behind my words. If my daughter disapproved of my girlfriend, then she wouldn't be my girlfriend. Paisley is number one in my life, and she's got to approve of someone that I have in our lives. That realization hits me square in the chest. How with past women, I never even dreamed of introducing them to her, but with Lindsay, I didn't even second guess it. I just did and never looked back. Maybe that was my conscience helping me out.

"Are we eating outside?" Lindsay asks, poking her head out the sliding glass door.

"Sure, the weather is nice," I reply. "Hey, P, can you pull out the cushions for the table?" I ask Paisley. She hops off the chair she was on and opens the deck box, pulls out the cushions, and places them on the three chairs we'll sit at for dinner. Once she gets them all situated, she steps inside and grabs the little container I keep stocked with napkins and condiments for ease of carrying, and places it on the center of the table.

"All done, what now?" Paisley asks, standing a few feet from the grill so she doesn't accidentally touch it and burn herself.

"That's all I have for you to do. You can poke your head back inside and see if Lindsay needs help with anything." She opens the door, but before she can ask Lindsay, Buckley comes racing out the door, almost knocking into her.

"Go throw the ball for Buckley," I suggest. She picks one up off the deck and heads down onto the grass. Her cast hasn't really slowed her down these past few weeks. Once she got past the first day or two after the accident, she was basically back to her usual, carefree self, just with a few bumps and bruises and, of course, the broken arm, as takeaways from the accident.

"Smells good out here." Lindsay's voice pulls my attention away from watching Paisley throwing the ball for Buckley.

"Sure does. Have you made these packets before?"

"Not this specific recipe, but I've made similar ones.

The sauce for this one was a recipe, so hopefully, it's good."

"I'm sure it will be perfect," I tell her as I take the food off of the grill, placing it all on a platter. "Paisley," I call out. "Dinner time," I tell her once she stops and looks my way.

I take the platter to the table a few feet from the grill. Before I sit down, I duck inside and grab Buckley's food bowl, getting it ready so that we don't have a dog begging for food while we're eating.

"Buckley, come," I call out, standing next to the sliding glass door. "Good boy, now sit," I tell him, and he obeys. I place his bowl down, giving him a look to stay put until I tell him otherwise. I don't make him wait long. "Okay, you can eat," I tell him, and he dives right into the food, lapping it up as only a dog can.

"So, my cousin is coming for Thanksgiving this year!" Lindsay says excitedly as we eat our dinner.

"Awesome, when is she coming in?" I know that she was hopeful that Reese would be able to come back for the holidays.

"She's going to fly in on the Tuesday before and stay for, like, ten days. Austin can only be here for two of them because then he's out on a road trip, but at least they're coming, and I get to see them!"

"That's great," I tell her. "Speaking of Thanksgiving, I was thinking today about it and what we're doing. I'd kind of like to spend it together, if we can. Hit up both of our family's dinners, if possible."

"What is your family's tradition? Early or late dinner?"

"Well, it's never really set in stone because of me and Dad's work schedule. There have been many years that we've celebrated on a different day because one or both of us were working. In the last few years, we've eaten at a normal dinner time because I've had to work."

"Do you know if that's the plan this year?" Lindsay asks.

"I haven't asked Mom what her plans were, but I can. What does your family do?"

"We've always eaten at two o'clock on the dot. That was something my Nana started, and Mom had continued the tradition on, when she took over hosting when Nana no longer could."

"I'll get Mom to have ours around six, then. We can go to your parents' place for your family's get together and then head to my parents' around five," I suggest.

"Sounds perfect to me. Will Paisley be with you this year? Or how do you guys handle holidays with her?" she asks.

"We usually split the day if I'm off, and if I'm not, then she's with Lilly on the holiday and with me on whatever day my family ends up picking. So, she'll probably have to miss your family's, and we can pick her up on the way to my parents'."

"That works. Mom will probably give us crap for not bringing her with us, but will understand. She likes having little kids around, so she's going to be so excited that Reese, Austin, and Nicole are coming; well, she'll mostly be excited about Nicole, but ya know she can't be there without Reese and Austin." She laughs at her own statement.

"How old is she?" I ask.

"A little over a year."

"That's a fun age."

"Reese says she's into everything now that she's walking and running around."

"How do they handle having a baby out on the road when she's touring?"

"She hasn't done a full tour yet since Nicole was born, just a few shows here and there. If Austin hasn't been able to go with her, then her mom flies out to be there to take care of Nicole when Reese is busy."

"I can't imagine having to juggle a kid and being on the road, so I don't blame her for not wanting to be on tour right now."

"Yeah, she's just enjoying being a mom, for now. She's been so go-go-go for so many years now, has definitely earned the longer break."

"So, back to turkey day. As long as my family can pull off the evening time, does that plan sound like it will work for you?" I ask.

"Sounds perfect to me," Lindsay says, leaning over and kissing my cheek.

"Daddy?" Paisley pulls my attention her way.

"Yes?"

"Can I take a bath with Buckley?" she asks, and I can't stop the bark of laughter that comes out.

"No, that's not something we do. When Buckley needs a bath, we can give him one, but it wouldn't be when you're in the tub. We'll actually take him to a special place to give him one. Kind of like when you go get your hair cut. Buckley will do the same," I explain to Paisley.

"Okay," she grumbles. I've obviously burst her bubble and whatever plans she'd cooked up in her mind.

"Sorry, honey. It just isn't a good idea. Plus, he'd make you all dirty, which is the exact opposite of what's supposed to happen when you take a bath."

She heavily sighs again as my words sink in. "Can I have another hot dog?" she asks, changing the subject as only a kid can.

"Of course," I tell her as I grab a bun from the bag and place a hot dog in it before covering it with ketchup, just the way she likes it.

"Thank you," she says as I hand over the hot dog.

"You're welcome."

"Lindsay, is it time to show Daddy our surprise yet?" Paisley asks.

Lindsay looks between the two of us before nodding her head. She pushes back from the table and they both head inside, coming back out with a cherry pie.

"We made your favorite dessert!" Paisley exclaims as she beams next to Lindsay.

"That looks delicious!"

We finish up dessert, enjoying the mild weather that is allowing us to sit outside tonight. After the long shift I just had, I needed an easy night like this with my girls.

"Dish," Lindsay says as soon as I drop onto the couch next to her. I just finished tucking Paisley in, and she's been waiting not so patiently to hear about my messed up day.

I stand up and move things off the couch, then lay back down, placing my head on Lindsay's lap. Her fingers go straight to my hair as she runs them through the strands, slightly massaging my scalp. I moan in pleasure, the feeling attempting to lull me to sleep.

"Quit stalling, mister," she teases me, poking me in the shoulder. "I'll stop massaging you if you don't start talking."

"It was the weirdest fucking call I think I've ever been on, and that's saying something." I shudder, the visual of what we walked in on today, coming back to me.

"Okay..." She draws out the word. "Explain."

"All dispatch said was a male who was stuck in his house. That happens more than you'd think, but a lot of times, it's an elderly person who's fallen and can't get up."

"I take it this wasn't an older person?" She smiles down at me, obviously picking up on my discomfort and enjoying it a little too much.

"Nope. We walked in, and the wife pointed us towards the bedroom."

"Go on," Lindsay giggles.

I rub a hand over my eyes, trying like hell to make the feeling of walking into that room go away. "The guy was a good three hundred pounds, spread eagle with his hands and legs chained to the four posts of the bed. He was dressed in a lace teddy with a matching thong. The 'clothes' hid absolutely nothing to cover *anything* from our view. The bed was covered with sex toys, and the wife couldn't get the locks undone that were securing him to the bed. We had to cut him out of them."

"Oh my god!" Lindsay guffaws and falls over in her fit of laughter. "How?" she starts to question, but gets nothing else out because she's laughing so hard.

"As I said, the most messed up call I think I've ever been on. I showered as soon as we got back to the station, yet I still don't feel clean after that call."

Lindsay is wheezing; she's laughing so hard, which causes me to follow suit. I can definitely see a sliver of humor from the situation, and feel bad for the guy. I'm sure he's feeling quite embarrassed, but shit, that isn't the kind of call I signed up to go out on when I joined the academy.

"What did he do once you guys had him cut out?"

"Grabbed a robe and covered up, then tried to offer us his hand to shake as he thanked us profusely."

"Are you shitting me?" she barks.

"Nope. Not one bit."

"Damn. I don't know if I'd have been able to keep a straight face during all of that."

"Oh, trust me. It wasn't a laughing matter when we were there. Not one bit."

"I've had my share of weird things inside people's bodies that 'get lost' and we've had to remove in the ER," Lindsay says, sitting back up.

"I don't even want to know." I shudder just thinking of what she could have dealt with.

"This one time..." she starts.

"Stop!" I put my hands up, one laying over her mouth lightly to stop her from saying anything else. "I don't want to know." I laugh.

"Oh, come on, I've got some fun ones." She winks.

"How about you just keep those stories to yourself and come kiss me instead," I suggest.

"Now that I can get on board with," she tells me, leaning over and pressing her lips to mine.

17

LINDSAY

"Hey, babe, it's time to go!" I call down the hall to Tucker. We're due at my parents' house in just a little bit, and I want to get there early so I can finally see my cousin and her family. They arrived earlier this week, but I was working, and she was spending as much time as she could with our Nana. Reese and Nana always had a super close relationship, so I know it's hard on her to no longer live around here.

"I'm coming," Tucker calls out as he struts down the hall, looking like sex on legs. That man makes me weak in the knees every time my eyes land on him, and today is no different.

"You sure were an hour ago," I quip.

"And whose mind is in the gutter?" he asks, stalking over to me. His hands circle around my torso, pulling me flush against him. I suck in a deep breath, getting a lung full of his cologne. The spicy smell tickles my nose slightly since it's so potent at the moment, but I love it on him.

"Like you wouldn't have said the same damn thing if the roles were reversed?" I ask, running my hands up his chest.

"You've got me there," he admits, bringing his lips to mine for a quick kiss. "I'm ready when you are," he tells me as he pulls back. His hand drops to my ass, giving it a quick squeeze.

"I'm ready, just need to grab the bag of things for Buckley," I tell him. Since we're going to be gone all day, we're bringing Buckley with us today. Paisley will be excited to have him with us at Tucker's parents' house later, and he'll fit right in amongst the huge crowd at my parents' this afternoon.

"You grab that, and I'll load Buckley up."

I quickly grab the bag with some food and his bowls, along with a few treats to have on hand for the day. I follow him out of the house, hopping up into the truck. He hits the garage button after getting settled in himself, and we're off to my parents' house.

"Hello! Happy Thanksgiving!" I call out as we come through the side door of my parents' house.

"Lindsay!" my cousin calls out from the living room. "You made it, finally!"

"How was the flight?" I ask, wrapping her in a hug once we reach each other. She's got a toddling Nicole following behind her, so I break our embrace and sweep up my little cousin into my arms. I bury my nose in her neck, sucking in that baby smell as I snuggle her in tightly. Her hands go to my hair, grabbing fists full. "Owe," I mumble into her neck.

"Nicole, no pulling hair." I hear Reese try and correct

her daughter and then feel her hands releasing my hair as Reese opens her little fists.

"Thanks, I don't need to have two bald spots just yet," I say, laughing at the baby.

"It's why I keep my hair up in a messy bun, most days," she says, smiling at her daughter in my arms.

"Hey, Reese, good to see you," Tucker greets her, and I almost forgot he was with me. I was so excited to see her that I completely left him in my dust.

"Tucker." She smiles at him behind me. "Thanks for putting that smile on this girl," she tells him, as if I'm not right here between them.

"My pleasure," he tells her, his hand sliding along my back and stopping on my hip. His words are like a lightning bolt straight to my center; the meaning of them can be interpreted in multiple ways.

"I'm sure it is," Reese muses, not missing his innuendo.

"I see the teenage boy humor is a family trait," he quips, and it has all of us laughing.

"The guys are in the living room waiting on the first football game of the day to come on," Reese tells Tucker. "And the mothers are all in the kitchen," she tells me.

"Does that mean that we're expected in the kitchen?" I ask, rolling my eyes. Reese and I always found excuses to not be in the kitchen on holidays. We wanted to be out playing or talking about boys.

"I got a pass since little miss, here, is being clingy and is more of a hazard in the kitchen today, especially with so many people in there working. So, we've been hanging out in the living room watching the balloons on parade.

"Is she boycotting Austin?" I ask, knowing that she's usually a daddy's girl.

"I think the combination of the flight, cutting three new teeth, and a messed up schedule all together has her just off today. Add in all the extra hands around that want to hold her, and she's just had enough."

"I don't blame her one bit," I say, snuggling Nicole a little tighter. "I'll keep them all away from you, sweetheart," I tell the baby. She just squawks her approval and then leans out of my arms and reaches for Reese.

"Go find a spot to claim in the living room; I'll be in there shortly. I'm just going to poke my head into the kitchen, first," I tell Tucker, kissing his cheek before I turn for the kitchen.

"Don't worry, no one will bite," I hear Reese tell Tucker as she heads back into the living room herself.

"I'm here," I say over the noise of the busy kitchen. My mom, aunts, and two grandmothers are all in here—the grandmothers at the table, where they're working on the pies for later.

"Oh, good! I'm glad that you finally graced us with your presence. Where is that man of yours that has been monopolizing all your time lately?" Mom asks.

"In the living room with everyone else," I tell her, accepting the cheek kiss she offers since her hands are covered in the dough for the rolls.

"I guess that's acceptable," she huffs, rolling dough around in a circle before punching it down.

"How's work going?" my nana asks from her spot at the table.

"Keeping me busy, but good. How's life at the nursing home?"

"Oh, you know how it is, our own little drama-filled life." She laughs. Some of the stories she's told us of the antics some of the residents pull are downright hilarious. They make teenagers look mild with some of the sneaking around they do.

"I'm glad to hear that nothing's changed. What would keep you entertained if it wasn't for the shenanigans everyone pulls over there." I walk over and give both of my grandmothers a hug and kiss on their cheeks.

"Good to see you, child," Nana says, patting my cheek. "You need to bring that hunky man of yours over to visit me. I've got to talk to him, see if he earns the Nana seal of approval," she says, looking around me and into the living room. I look over my shoulder, my eyes immediately finding Tucker's. The edge of his lips tugs up when our eyes meet, and my heart does a little skip in my chest. He's talking with my dad and cousin-in-law. I can't hear what exactly they're talking about, but it must be interesting, the way they're all using their hands to help them discuss the topic at hand.

"I'll see what I can do to remedy that," I tell her. "Our schedules don't always line up, but I'll make it a priority. He's a good one, I promise," I tell her, bringing my attention back to the table.

"He'd better be, or that daddy of yours won't take too kindly to him breaking your heart."

"I'm a big girl, Nana. If my heart is broken, I can mend it without Dad going all caveman overprotective on a guy."

She hums, but I know that just means she's dropping the subject before it gets out of hand.

I visit awhile longer with the women in my family. Thankfully, they've already handled all the prepping of the food, so I'm not needed in the kitchen. I wander out and find Tucker on the couch, the guys all visit as they watch the football game. Austin sits on the floor as Nicole climbs all over him, as if he's her personal jungle gym.

"Hey, Austin," I greet him as I take a seat on the floor in front of Tucker and next to Austin.

"How's it going?" he asks, Nicole crawling over him to get to me.

"Can't complain. How about you?"

"Same. Nice to get away for a few days, even with it still being early in the season, a few days away from the daily grind is always appreciated."

"How's it looking this year?" I ask, referring to his season.

"I think we've got potential, for sure. A few newer guys are still learning their place on the team and that chemistry that comes from playing together for years."

"Makes sense; I'm sure you'll get there. How much longer do you think you'll play?" I ask.

"That's the million-dollar question, if I've ever been asked one." He chuckles. "Honestly, I hope for another seven, maybe eight seasons, ten if I'm fortunate."

"Oh, wow. I didn't think that guys played for that long professionally."

"It just really depends on how old they were when they started in the league and how lucky they are with injuries. Someone might take a bad hit early on in their career, and that's it. They're done for good. Knock on wood, I've been pretty lucky and haven't had any major injuries thus far in my career. If I can keep it that way and take care of my body during the offseason, then I should be able to keep playing for the foreseeable future. Now, depending on Reese and her stuff, I might decide to retire early and follow her around, being the stay at home dad and house husband so that she can go out and kick ass making music and entertaining the masses. Lord knows she's more famous than I am, and her career will last a hell of a lot longer than mine will."

"I love it that you'd be willing to give up your career so she can focus on hers."

"I know who's the boss in my marriage." He chuckles.

"I am not the boss," Reese interjects. "And you're not retiring anytime soon," she tells him, trying like hell to be stern. He just laughs at his wife, pulling her in for a kiss. Nicole stands up and leans in, attempting to kiss both of them at the same time, and I can't help but swoon at how cute of a family they make. Being around Nicole has my mind wandering to what it would be like to have a baby. I already know that Tucker is an amazing dad to Paisley; I can only imagine how amazing he would be with a baby. We haven't really brought up the topic of wanting more kids. It's probably something we should at least discuss if our relationship continues the way it has over the last couple of months.

The day is filled with conversations and food. So much food. It amazes me how tiring family events can be but how fulfilled I feel after leaving them. Tucker fit right in with my family, which I expected him to do. It wasn't like anyone in attendance, except maybe Austin, didn't already know him, know who his family is and what he's like. If anything, I think that really helped make the day go by so much smoother. It wasn't that awkward first-time meeting that it could have easily been if I'd been dating someone else.

"READY FOR ROUND TWO?" TUCKER ASKS, REACHING FOR my hand once we're on the road. Our first stop is to pick up Paisley from Mike's parents' house. With Lilly's broken leg still in a cast, she was in no shape to host their families for the holiday, so they went to her in-law's place.

"I was born ready," I tease. "And today is why yoga pants were invented—no bulky jeans cutting into me while I eat my weight in turkey and all the fixings. Plus, pie. I can't really say no to pie."

"You crack me up, you know that?" he laughs, bringing our clasped hands up to his lips as he presses them against the back of my hand.

"Hey, I'll cut a bitch if they try to get between me and my pie."

"Oh, I'm very aware. I almost lost a finger," he teases.

"Sorry about that. I'm not used to sharing my pie," I apologize. I almost stabbed him when he tried to steal some of my pie earlier.

"I know, now, to not come between you and the pie. I'll warn you, though, my dad is just as crazy about pie as you are, so don't be shocked if he already has pieces picked out of each one that he's already dubbing the winners and his slices."

"Got it, don't battle dad over pie."

Mike's parents live not far from my parents, so it doesn't take us long to arrive. I stay in the truck, along with Buckley, while Tucker goes up to the house to get Paisley.

"Hi, Paisley," I greet her as Tucker buckles her into her seat next to Buckley. He leans over, licking her face, causing her to giggle as he tries to clean the food off her face.

"Hi, Lindsay! Buckley, stop," she tells him, pushing him out of her face. He listens, settling back on the seat next to her. Once she's fully buckled, he drops his head on her lap, and she goes right to petting him.

"How's your day been so far?" Tucker asks as he pulls out of the packed driveway.

"So fun!" she exclaims. "I played and ate lots of food."

"Sounds like the perfect Thanksgiving!" I tell her. "We did the same thing at my parents' house. Are you ready for Nona and Papa's?"

"Yeah, but I'm not hungry. Do I have to have more turkey?" she questions.

"Only if you want to, but I'm sure that Nona has made your favorite potatoes," Tucker tells her.

"Okay." She sighs, and I can tell that she's already tired from today's events.

"Maybe the two of us can sneak away from everyone when we get to Nona and Papa's and take a little nap. I'm feeling tired," I offer, winking at Tucker to let him know that she might benefit from a short nap.

"Maybe." Paisley yawns as her head rests back against the edge of her seat. I can tell that her eyes are getting heavy as the car ride starts to lull her to sleep. Damn turkey, making people tired on Thanksgiving.

"I don't think she's going to last even until we make it to your parents'," I quietly tell Tucker.

"You're probably right about a nap not being a bad idea. Especially since we'll probably be here pretty late."

"I don't mind lying down with her for a little bit," I tell him, reiterating my offer.

"If she passes out before we get there, I can probably get her inside without her waking up. But if you need a nap, I won't stop you. Need you well rested for later." He smirks.

"Oh, really?" I quirk an eyebrow at him. "And who jumped whom this morning?"

"You know you can't resist me," he throws right back at me. He's not wrong, but I like to think that the feeling is mutual and that we're both just as gone for each other.

"And she's out," I tell Tucker as he pulls up to his parents' house.

"You get Buckley, and I'll get Paisley," he tells me, shutting the truck off.

"Sounds like a plan." I jump down, then open the back door. Buckley hops out, heading straight for the house.

I hold the screen door open for Tucker to walk through, a sleeping Paisley in his arms. He carries her back to one of the bedrooms and successfully transfers her without her waking up. Poor girl is tuckered out.

We head toward the noise from his family, all gathered around in the living room, kitchen, and dining room areas. Much like my family was, the women are congregated together in the kitchen, while the men are watching the football game on TV, or even outside playing their own football game.

"Hey, Mom," Tucker greets her, accepting the hug she pulls him into.

"Where's my Paisley girl?" she asks, looking around him for her granddaughter.

"Asleep on the bed. She passed out on the drive over here," he explains.

"Oh, sweet child. She must have had fun today for her to take a nap so willingly," Donna muses.

"My thoughts exactly." Tucker chuckles, stepping back from his mother's embrace.

"Happy Thanksgiving, Lindsay," Donna greets me.

"Happy Thanksgiving, thanks for having me."

"Of course, dear. The more, the merrier." She pulls me into a hug of my own, and I see the smile that fills Tucker's face. I know his parents mean everything to him, just as Paisley does, so to know that having me here means something to him makes it that much more of an important day.

"I DON'T KNOW HOW WE MADE IT HOME WITHOUT SOMEONE wheeling me in," I joke, dropping down on the bed. The day was long, filled with so much love, laughter, and a ton of food. "I'm going to be full for the next week; I ate so much."

"I'm sure you'll be out rummaging through the fridge, looking for pie, come morning," Tucker smirks, tossing his shirt into the hamper.

"Well, duh, there is always room for pie, especially for breakfast. Plus, it's got fruit in it, so, therefore, it is healthy," I say, doing my best to keep a straight face, but failing when he gives me an *oh really* look.

"Sure, we'll go with the fruit, so healthy, bit," he teases before ducking into the bathroom.

I lay back on the pillow, being lazy and not getting myself up to get ready for bed; thankfully, I have tomorrow off so I can sleep in and get a few things done before returning to work on Saturday.

"So, are you going to get ready for bed or just lay there like a bump on a log?" Tucker asks as he steps out of the bathroom in nothing but his tight boxer briefs.

"But I'm comfortable," I pout, rolling over and off the bed. I head toward the bathroom, but Tucker intercepts me, pulling me into his practically naked body.

"Thank you for today," he says, cupping my cheeks. "It was my favorite Thanksgiving I can think of in a long time."

"All I did was eat and visit," I tell him.

"You did more than that. But I'm not referring to those parts of the day. I'm talking about all the little moments. Sharing our lives together, how we easily slip into one another's families. That isn't always easy, but we've made it easy. Thank you for always looking out for Paisley. She really does look up to you, and that's important to me as her father. I've never had a woman in my life—or hers—that didn't realize the importance that she plays in my life and know that she's my number one priority and be okay with that."

"Tucker," I sigh his name. "Of course, Paisley is your number one. I'd judge you if she wasn't. You've done a great job being her dad, and don't let that ever change. She's lucky to have you and Lilly as her parents."

He pulls me in tighter, until his lips cover mine. What starts out slow quickly builds into roaming hands, nips and sucking, dueling tongues, and clashing teeth.

"Let me get ready for bed," I mumble against his lips. "Then we can continue this in bed."

"Make it fast, woman," he says, smacking my ass as I turn for the bathroom.

I appease him by rushing through my bedtime routine so I can meet him back in bed. He's lying on top of the blankets when I emerge from the bathroom, naked and stroking his cock as he watches for me.

"Mhmm..." I hum my approval. I stand at the doorway for a few seconds, waiting to see what he does. I had the same thoughts and stripped while I was in the bathroom. His eyes roaming over my naked body is like a branding on my skin. He might as well be running his fingertips up and down my skin the way his eyes bore into me.

"Get your sexy ass over here," he says, patting the bed next to him, all while still stroking his cock.

I saunter as sexily as I can over to the bed. When I reach the foot of it, I place a knee against the mattress and crawl up; as I pass over his groin, I drop my head, licking the length of his cock from root to tip before I circle his crown and sucking him deep into my mouth.

"Fuuuuck," he groans, his head thunking against the

headboard as I work his cock over. Tucker slips one hand into my hair, gathering it to keep it from falling into my way as I bob up and down, sucking him over and over as my fist and mouth move in tandem.

"Linds," he warns, tapping my shoulder. "Stop, please," he grits out between clenched teeth. I pop off his cock, but don't stop stroking him with my fist.

"Something wrong?" I cheekily ask.

"I'm *not* coming in your mouth tonight," he tells me, flipping me onto my back. His lips land between my breasts as he nips his way to my left nipple. He sucks it into his mouth, laving at it until it hardens into a tight bud. He moves to the right, doing the same thing to that one while one hand slides down my torso and through my folds.

"Yes!" I cry out, my back bowing slightly as his fingers graze over my clit. I'm so desperate for his touch and a release. He slides two fingers inside, twisting them until he finds that magic spot—my body trembles as he works me up, building that release that we both so desperately want.

Tucker pulls his fingers from my core, causing me to whimper at the loss. "Why did you stop?" I pout. I was not ready for him to stop.

"Because you're not coming on my fingers tonight," he tells me as he positions himself above me. I watch as he fists his cock, stroking it a few times before he lines himself up with my entrance. His lips land on mine as he thrusts inside, until he's fully seated and balls deep.

My cry of complete pleasure is swallowed by his kiss.

Our kiss matches the intensity and rhythm he sets,

pistoning his hips and building up the ultimate release. My body trembles as it falls over the edge, my orgasm taking hold of my entire body, from the curling of my toes to my fingertips that claw at Tucker's back, leaving a mark on his skin like he's left on my heart.

His pleasure-filled grunts and satisfied smirk tell me that he's feeling just as good as I am. His release comes hard and fast, filling me with one last snap of his hips against my own. "Damn, baby," he pants, pinning me to the bed. My legs stay wrapped around his hips, my ankles locking behind his back as we both recover.

Once he's caught his breath, he pulls back slightly, looking down at me still pinned beneath him. "You good?" he asks sweetly.

"Never been better," I tell him, meaning every word.

The smile that fills his face could light up a room. He brushes a few strands of hair out of my face before he kisses me sweetly. No urgency, no need to deepen the kiss. He pulls back again, leaving just enough space between us that we can easily look into each other's eyes. "I love you," he whispers.

"I love you, too," I tell him as I feel tears slide from my eyes and down the sides of my cheeks and into my hairline.

"Why the tears?" Tucker asks, wiping them away.

"Because I've never told someone that and felt it so deeply. I thought I knew what love was before, but it was nothing like what I feel with you." He doesn't answer me with words; I don't need them. He kisses me again, this time a little more urgency in his kiss.

18

TUCKER

THE PAST MONTH HAS FLOWN BY. I CAN'T BELIEVE Christmas is already upon us, but here it is.

"Daddy?" Paisley calls for me from the other room.

"Yes?" I answer, walking into the living room.

"We need your help," she says, doing her best to reach the top of the tree.

"I'll pick you up; just give me a second," I tell her, setting down the steaming mugs of hot chocolate. We didn't get a tree set up until last week, just due to crazy schedules, and I've held off on decorating it until Paisley, Lindsay, and I could all do it together. It just so happens that today, three days before Christmas, is that day. So, we decided to make a day of it. Decorate the tree and house; we're going to try our hand at baking some cookies later, and round out the night with some takeout and a movie night with the classic *The Santa Clause.*

I pick Paisley up, setting her on my shoulders and handing her the ornament she wanted to place higher on the tree than she could reach with the stool. It takes her about twenty more minutes to get all the ornaments on the tree with Lindsay and my help, but once it's done, it looks perfect. I plug in the lights and step back to see it glow in the front window. "You ladies did a great job," I praise them both.

"You helped, too; we can't take all the credit," Lindsay says. I hold an arm open, and she tucks herself right into my side. With Paisley on the other, we all stand back and admire our handiwork.

"It looks beautiful," Lindsay agrees. "Are we ready to make some cookies now?" she asks both Paisley and me.

"Cookies!" Paisley cheers and bolts for the kitchen.

"I'll take that as a yes." She laughs.

I pull Lindsay into a hug, tucking my hands into her back pockets and cupping her ass. It's a delectable one that I can't keep my hands off of. "I'll clean up the boxes and stuff, and then be in to help the two of you," I tell her, before sweeping some hairs off her face and tucking them behind her ear. I drop a quick kiss to her lips before stepping away. If I'd have allowed the kiss to go longer or deeper, I don't know that I'd have had the willpower to stop kissing her. We've been apart so much the last few weeks, due to our conflicting schedules, that I need that connection with her. She grounds me, and I almost feel lost without her.

"Sounds good; we'll be waiting," she tells me before going to join my daughter in the kitchen. I stay put, listening to them talking as Lindsay reads off the ingredients they need for the cookies they're starting with. As they begin pulling everything out, I get a move on it so that I can join them sooner than later.

"The Cookie Monster has arrived," I announce as I enter the kitchen a little while later. The mixer is whipping something up, and the oven is beeping, alerting us that it is up to temperature. "Who's ready to feed me?" I ask. I can't help but laugh as I take in the picture before me. I slip my phone out of my pocket and snap a couple of pictures of my girls together. Paisley has probably as much flour on her as the bowl does. But the smiles on their faces as they measure and bake together hit me straight in the chest.

"We don't have anything for you, yet, but just be patient," Lindsay tells me, looking up and flashing me a smile.

"Can I do anything to help?" I offer.

"Not yet. We're still mixing everything together. Maybe once we're ready to scoop, you can help."

"Okay," I agree and pull out a stool to sit down on at the counter. I just watch Lindsay and Paisley and how easily they work together. A stranger looking in the windows would never know that they weren't mother and daughter. That we were not the happy, perfect, little American family. Lindsay might not be Paisley's mom, but this is the family I want, the one I need in my life. The momentum of that reality hits me square in the heart. I've known I love this woman for weeks now; I've told her that as many times as I could since that first time. I've known that we were definitely working our way toward these serious conversations. Marriage, kids, life, moving in together, but I didn't realize that they could happen so quickly. But in this exact instance, this moment is one of clarity. I want this, all of it and more.

Even with the epiphany, I know that trying to pull off a proposal for Christmas isn't in the cards. I need time to plan the perfect proposal, shop for the perfect ring, and, most importantly, have a little chat with Lindsay's parents and with Paisley. I know she loves Lindsay, but I need to make sure my daughter is truly okay with me marrying someone. I know that it seems weird that I'd run something like that past my five-year-old, but this is her life, too, and I need to know that she's just as happy with things as I am.

"Earth to Tucker." Lindsay waves a hand in front of my face. "You okay?" she asks, the worry evident in the crease of her brow.

"Yeah." I shake my head, as if that could jar the plans already spinning in my mind.

"Did you want a bite of the cookie dough?" she asks, holding up a spoon.

"Of course. Isn't that the best part?" I ask.

Lindsay scoops out a spoonful of the dough and hands it over. "Mhmm, this is good!" I tell them as I eat it. Lindsay helps Paisley with a scoop as she plunks down balls of the dough on a cookie sheet. Lindsay must have brought a few things over, since I don't recognize many of these items, and I know for sure I didn't have some of them.

"Need any help?" I offer it again.

"I think we've got it, for now."

"Okay." I'm content just sitting back and watching the two of them work together. I sneak a few more candid pictures of them together, Lindsay wiping some flour off of Paisley's cheek, the two of them looking in the window at the cookies as they bake.

"Daddy, can I have a cookie when they are done?" Paisley asks as the timer ticks down.

"Maybe once they cool. If you try to eat one right away, it might burn your mouth."

"How about we have some with a glass of milk once they cool," Lindsay suggests.

"Yes!" Paisley cheers. She hops off the stool she was on so she could help. Now that they have a sheet of cookies in the oven and the second sheet all scooped and ready to go in, so doesn't have anything to keep her busy. Lindsay, on the other hand, keeps busy as she starts to bustle around, cleaning up and putting things away.

"Are you just making the one kind today?" I ask, sneaking another bite of dough.

"I wanted to make another batch, but we'll see how we're doing on time. I don't want to be baking all day and miss the movie," Lindsay says.

"Sounds good, sure there isn't anything I can help with?" I ask, coming around the counter and pressing against Lindsay's back as she stands at the kitchen sink. Her little apron tied in the back, bare feet on the floor. Her hair is pulled up in a messy bun on the top of her head, and I can't stop kissing along her exposed neck as my arms box around her and I rest my hands against the counter.

She leans into my touch, her ass rubbing against my cock and causing it to spring to life. That wouldn't usually be a problem, but with my daughter just a few feet away and my sweatpants not hiding anything, I pull away slightly, needing to cool things down. "Later," I whisper for only Lindsay to hear.

"You can dry after I wash," she tells me, handing me a dishtowel. She gets to work filling the sink with some soapy water and washing the measuring cups, mixing bowls, and everything else they used in the process of baking.

"All right, who's ready for some cookies and milk and a movie?" Lindsay asks about a half-hour later. All the cookies are baked and cooling, and the kitchen is clean with everything except the cooling rack washed and put away. Besides the container filled to the brim with cookies and the smell lingering, you'd never know the mess that was in here just an hour ago.

"Yes!" Paisley calls out, and turns for the fridge to grab the gallon of milk from the door. I pull down three mugs, setting them on the counter so I can fill them up.

"Here's two cookies for you, and two for Daddy, and two for me," Lindsay tells Paisley, setting each of our cookies out on napkins.

"Let's take them out to the living room and snuggle in for the movie," I suggest. I grab Paisley's mug of milk so that she doesn't spill it as she bounces to the living room, Buckley, on her heels as she goes. I don't know why I dragged my heels for so long on getting a dog, but Buckley has been a great addition to our family. They're like two peas in a pod.

"Daddy, is Santa Claus going to come to your house?"

"I don't see why he wouldn't."

"Will he also go to Mommy's?"

"I'm sure he'll stop there, as well. He's got to leave

presents for your brother, after all, and you never know, he might leave presents for you at both houses." I try my best to give her an answer that won't lead to a ton more questions. I'd love for her to have the magic of Christmas for a few more years before she stops believing.

"Okay." She's, apparently, appeased with my answer and flops back on the couch; Buckley curled up next to her as we watch the movie. I can't think of a better day. Downtime with my girls. Both cuddled up with me on the couch as we spend quality time together.

19

LINDSAY

Four months later

I walk around the lake outside the hospital, the crisp spring air filling my lungs as I go. I can't believe we've already made it to spring. Tucker's birthday is next week, and I've been trying to plan a surprise party for him with all our friends. He's been working like crazy lately, as they've been short-staffed.

"Do you have everything in place for the party next weekend?" Allison asks as we start our second lap.

"As far as I know. Everyone has been informed of the place and time. Easy enough, since it's just at Joe's."

"Do you think he has any idea you've been planning something?"

"I don't, but if he figures it out beforehand, it won't be the end of the world. Just thought it would be a nice thing to do for him. He's always doing things for everyone else; I wanted him to feel special, for once."

"Plus, who doesn't like a good party?" Allison asks.

"Exactly. And I need a night out. It feels like we haven't been out in months. I need a night to just dance the stress away."

"Right there with you, sister," Allison agrees.

"So, tell me how things are with Lee?"

"We are talking again; I think the break was needed. Even if it did suck for a while. But he's been open to my side of things, said he's willing to give things a try."

"That's good. Tucker said something last night about him being in a much better mood for the last couple of days. Figured it had something to do with you."

I look over at my best friend and see a ghost of a smile spread across her face, along with a blush.

"You slept with him, didn't you?" I ask as I just shake my head.

"Maybe," she says, and I'm not used to the embarrassment coming from Allison. She's always been a what you see is what you get kind of woman, who doesn't take shit from anyone and speaks her mind. "Okay, yes. I gave in, and holy shit, Linds. That man knows how to do things that I'd never dreamed of doing."

"Good for you!" I tell her, trying to make her feel comfortable telling me whatever she wants to share. "Just make sure you make him work for it a smidge."

"I've got that part covered," she says.

"So, the make-up sex was good, then?"

"It was phenomenal; there was no good about it. Like, rock my world, I don't know how I'm standing or walking today kind of make-up sex."

"Good for you."

"What about you and Tucker, things still in the honeymoon stage?"

"I think so; I mean, our schedules kind of suck, but we make the best of the time we do get. We're explosive when we're together. I don't know if it's because of our limited time, especially alone time, but I swear, when we're together, he's always got to be touching me in some way. It's cute most of the time, but others, I'm just like, dude, stop touching me. He gets all pouty when I tell him to back it up a step or two."

"Oh, men. Can't live with them, can't live without them." Allison laughs.

"Ain't that the truth." I laugh along with her.

"Have you guys talked about moving in together? I know you already spend all the nights he's home at his house, so wouldn't it be easier to just combine houses, at this point?"

"He's brought the idea up. Suggested I rent out my house rather than go straight to selling it, and that's a good idea, but we haven't really talked more than just surface conversation about it. Maybe after his birthday, I'll bring it up again. I could spend a month or so really sorting through all my things and downsizing. Then, come late spring, it should be ready for renters or to be sold."

"I'd come to help you when you need it."

"Thanks, I'll definitely need all the help I can get. De-junking is never a fun process, I've found," I tell her as we lap back around to the parking lot.

"Thanks for getting my butt outside today. I needed this," Allison says as we make it back to our cars.

"I needed it just as much. The fresh air did me wonders."

"Do you want to get a head start on some organizing today? I don't have anything pressing to do, so I could come help, if you wanted," Allison offers. I love my best friend to death, and she knows just when to step in to motivate me.

"I guess so. We can pick up some lunch on our way and then start in one room and see how far we get."

"Perfect, subs sound okay?" she suggests.

"Yeah, I could go for a sub. I'll meet you over at Pete's?" I ask, knowing there is nowhere else in town that makes better subs than Pete's.

"Like you even have to ask?" She laughs.

I LOOK AROUND MY SPARE ROOM, PILES ALREADY FORMING after an afternoon filled with sorting through things. I'm slightly shocked at how much ended up in the black trash bags to just go out to the curb. I didn't realize I had that much junk stored away. I've also got a nice pile of stuff set aside to take to donate, and another pile of things I'm going to try and sell.

"If you give me your phone, I'll start snapping pictures and uploading things to the marketplace," Allison offers.

"That'd be great," I say, tossing over my phone. She starts laying things out and snapping pictures. Occasionally asking what I think the price should be. Before I know it, she's got everything photographed and listed, and already some people on their way to look at or purchase items.

"I might have to pay you a commission on everything that sells," I joke after she shows me yet another item is pending.

"Hmmm, I should have thought of that earlier." She giggles. "Tell you what, you buy the first round of drinks next weekend, and we'll call it even."

"You're so good to me. It's a deal," I tell her as someone knocks on the front door. We both head out to see who it is. The young girl at my door is here to buy a few of the items.

"Thanks again!" she calls as she loads the items into her trunk. Just as she's pulling out, another car pulls in. This cycle continues for the next hour or so.

"I can't believe you sold all of that stuff so quickly. Why didn't I think of doing this earlier?" I ask Allison. I count the cash I've been stuffing in my pockets. I've made a few hundred bucks already, and we only tackled a few rooms in my house. I've more than made enough to cover a couple rounds of drinks for Tucker's party next weekend, so I say today was a huge success.

"Tucker is not going to know what to do with himself when you tell him you're ready to move in and have already condensed things down."

"I think he'll be A-okay with the idea. As it is, he tries to get me to sleep over at his house on the nights he's not home so that I'll be there when he gets home in the morning."

"See, he's going to be so on board with this idea. I'll

make sure he knows it was my idea to light a fire under your ass once you guys are ready for it."

"You do that." I laugh and my cell pings with a text notification from none other than Tucker.

Tucker: Hey, baby, how's your day?

Lindsay: Good, Allison is over and helped me purge a bunch of things. I sold a ton of it on the marketplace already.

Tucker: Cool, are you going to be at my place when I get there in a few hours?

Lindsay: Do you want me to be? {winky face}

Tucker: Like that's even a question. If you're busy at your place, I can just come there.

Lindsay: Whatever works, I'm flexible.

Tucker: Yes, yes, you are. {devilish smirk}

Lindsay: You're incorrigible {kissy face} I'll be at your place by 6, sound good?

Tucker: See you then. Love you.

Lindsay: Love you too

"You are so gone for that man," Allison laughs from where she still stands a few feet from me.

"How'd you know it was Tucker?" I ask.

"Because of the way your face lit up, and that little smile that's still on it from whatever it was that he said to you."

"I can't explain it. I just get all these butterflies every time he calls or texts me while at work. Knowing he's thinking about me just, ah..." I screech, letting my hands go up and then slap against my thighs. "I just can't explain it."

"That's called love, m'dear. Don't let that feeling go; enjoy it. I'm so damn happy for the two of you," she says, pulling me in for a hug.

"I can only hope you find this kind of love for yourself," I mumble into her shoulder.

"I'll get there, and when I do, you can tell me the same thing."

"You're such a good best friend," I tell Allison. I really did hit the jackpot by having Allison in my life.

"All right, no more sappy shit. Let's get the bags of trash taken out, and then we can take a load over and drop it off at the donation collection place," she says, stepping back from our hug.

We get to work doing just that, and before I know it, my spare room is cleared out from all our piles.

20

TUCKER

"Hey, babe," I call out to Lindsay as I look at my watch. We're supposed to meet our friends at the bar tonight. I've been tipped off to the fact that she tried to plan a surprise birthday party for me—which I'm playing coy to knowing anything about—but little does she know, I've got plans of my own for tonight.

"Yeah?" she says, stepping out of the bedroom and spinning for me.

The vision in front of me takes my breath away. The white sweater she's got on gapes open in the back, leaving her back exposed. Her legs are encased in blue jeans that show off all her curves, especially that luscious ass that I can't get enough of.

"Fuck, you are hot," I tell her, holding a hand out for her to come to me as she closes the distance between us. I pull her in, being careful to not mess up her makeup as I capture her lips with mine. "Ready to go?" I ask against her lips a few minutes later.

"Yep, I just need to grab something from my car,

200

quick," she says, and I can see the excitement dancing in her eyes.

I follow her out of the house, locking up behind me. I pat my own pocket, making sure the ring is still where I placed it while she was getting ready and not paying attention to me.

"I know I told you we were only meeting Lee and Allison here, but that might not have been the full truth," Lindsay says, wringing her hands in her lap as I park my truck in the parking lot for Joe's Bar.

"Is that so?" I ask, quirking an eyebrow at her and doing my best to hold back my laughter.

"There might be a few others here, as well." She shrugs, a smile tugging at her lips.

"Well, then let's get inside and see who's here to cut loose tonight."

We walk into the bar, hand in hand, and immediately find our group of friends. It isn't hard to spot them, since stretched above the tables they're at is a big "Happy Birthday" banner, along with some streamers and balloons.

"Surprise!" everyone calls out as we reach the tables. I don't hold in my laughter, but not because they actually surprised me, but because of how many of them are actually in on *my* surprise for tonight, and not Lindsay's.

She turns to face me, her eyes bouncing between the group of guys from my truck at work, and me. "They told you about tonight, didn't they?" she finally asks, the humor evident in her question. Thankfully, it doesn't appear that she's mad that the surprise wasn't, in fact, a surprise.

"Sorry, Linds," Lee calls out. "He kind of figured it out

when he overheard one of the guys talking about it in the locker room after shift, earlier this week."

"And you just played along with my secrecy?" I asked.

"Pretty much. I knew that you wanted to surprise me, and I didn't want to take that away from you."

Lindsay blows out a big breath, the force of it causing her hair to move slightly. "I can't get anything passed you," she harrumphs only to start laughing. "Happy Birthday, Tuck. I love you," she says as I pull her into my arms.

"I love you, too, and thank you. It's the thought that counts. Now, let's get you out on that dance floor. I want to hold you close," I tell her, nipping at her lips before I take them in a kiss that gets our friends hooting behind us. I flip them the bird over her shoulder, not caring one bit that they're just egging us on.

I lead Lindsay out onto the dance floor just as "Rumor" by Lee Brice comes on. I pull her in close, listening to the words, and it's almost scary how much this song could be our story. How we kind of made things official right here on this exact dance floor. It's the reason I picked here to propose tonight. I thought circling back to where we made it all official was a romantic gesture, and my birthday makes her saying yes, the ultimate present she could give me.

"Come back to the table, birthday boy! It's time for some shots!" Lee calls out once the current song ends. We've danced to a handful of them already, and I'm ready for a drink or two.

"To this fucker, happy birthday, man," Lee calls out, holding up a shot glass. We all follow suit, clinking glasses before everyone slams their shot back and then onto the table. I lick the salt off my hand and quickly bite into the lime wedge to help with the burn from the tequila.

"Do you want something from the bar?" I lean down so I can speak right into Lindsay's ear, so she hears me over the noise filling the bar. It's a usual busy Saturday night, so the place is packed with more than just our rowdy group.

"I'll take a beer and a glass of water," she says.

"Be right back," I tell her, dropping a kiss to her lips before I step away and go grab our drinks. I need a little liquid courage in me to drop to one knee and ask her my ultimate question. I went a month or so ago and had lunch with her parents when she was at work. She doesn't know anything about that lunch, but it was important for me to get permission. They gave me their blessing without a second thought. Next was my daughter. I had to wait a little longer to talk to her about it, as I didn't want her spilling the beans before I could ask. When I spoke to her last weekend, she was over the moon and thought that I should have asked Lindsay that very night. I thought about it, making it a little private moment, but I already had things for tonight in the works, so I stuck with my original plan.

"A beer and water for milady." I hand over the drinks and kiss Lindsay's cheek before I down half of my own beer in just a couple gulps.

The ladies all let out a screech of excitement when "Country Girl" by Luke Bryan comes on. They all head for the dance floor and start shaking their asses as they cut it up dancing.

"You going to ask her, or are you chickening out?" Lee asks as we both watch them dancing.

"I'm not chickening out, asshole." I punch him in the shoulder. "I was planning on it when she comes back over here."

"Finish your beer and ask her. You know she's going to say yes, so the sooner you ask her, the sooner y'all can get the fuck out of here and celebrate." He smirks at me.

"Please don't think of my girl and sex ever again," I deadpan, staring my best friend down.

"Lighten up, asshole. It isn't like I said I was taking her to bed," he says and just laughs at me. He's got a point, but it doesn't change the fact that I'm protective over Lindsay, even if it is my best friend and someone that I know I could always trust around her.

"Did you have fun?" I ask once Lindsay returns to the table. She grabs the glass of water I brought her earlier and downs it. Her skin is shiny from the sheen of sweat covering it after dancing.

"Yes! I needed this tonight!" she says, wrapping her arms around me. I pull her in close, as if I'm going to kiss her, but I don't. I hold back just enough so that I can look her straight in the eyes.

"This feels almost like déjà vu," I tell her, looking around at our surroundings. "Being here with you, our friends in the background, me holding you like this. It seems like just yesterday we were in this exact spot physically, but in that limbo of do we or don't we see what this is between us. Thank you for taking the chance on me.

For loving me, loving my daughter. For making me hope and pray for more, for a family of my own." My words pour from my lips, and I can see tears start to form in her eyes. I wipe just under one as a tear escapes. I reach into my pocket and pull the ring out before I drop to my knee.

"Lindsay Rae Blackwood, will you do me the honor of being my wife?" I ask, holding up the ring to her. The bar has gone almost silent as everyone waits for her to answer. Her head nods frantically as the tears pour down her cheeks.

"Yes!" she finally says, and the entire place goes up in cheers. I slip the ring onto her finger and sweep her up into my arms as I stand up.

"I love you so damn much," I say before I press my lips against hers in a kiss.

"I love you. I can't believe you turned today into this," she says, pulling back and looking at me.

"You're my ultimate present, baby. You saying yes to me today was my one wish, and I'm the luckiest man in the world that you did."

"Take me home, fiancé. I've got one last birthday present for you." She gives me the sexiest smirk I think I've ever seen.

"Goodnight, everyone; my fiancée has instructed me to take her home," I call out to our group of friends. They let out another cheer as I lead Lindsay to my truck.

"Come," I tell her once we're home. We have the place to ourselves. Paisley's spending the night with my parents, and she took Buckley with her. She'd take him with her to her mom's if we'd let her, but Lilly doesn't, which is fine with me.

Lindsay follows me down the hall and into the bedroom, one that will soon be officially ours. We discussed it the last few days, and she's officially moving in and we'll put her place up for rent. Keep it as a little side income for us.

I link our fingers together, my thumb sliding over the ring I placed on it not that long ago. I flick the switch, turning on the bedside lamps to give us light to see one another.

I lead Lindsay over to the bed but don't move to let her sit down. Standing toe to toe, I slide my left hand up her neck, cupping her cheek as my fingers tangle in the hairs behind her ear. "I love you so fucking much, Linds. I can't wait to make a life with you. Have babies with you, fill this house with memories we make together as a family. Travel the world with you or just stay right here, sitting in the backyard around the fire pit. I want it all, baby, and I want it with only you." I kiss her, pressing my lips hard to hers, telling her so much with this kiss. Everything I can't think of to say with words, but that our bodies can tell each other.

"When?" she asks between kisses.

"When what, babe?" I ask, pulling back and looking down into her eyes.

"When do I get to marry you?" she asks, a smile on her lips as the words *marry you* come out.

"As soon as you want. I'm all yours," I tell her, picking her up and spinning us in a circle. "I'd marry you tonight if I thought you'd have gone along with it, but I also figured you'd want time to plan the perfect day. Pick out your perfect dress and plan everything to fit your dream. I want to give you that and so much more."

"How about this fall?" she asks, running her fingers through my hair.

"Done. We can look at a calendar tomorrow and pick a specific date."

"How about the third Saturday in October?" she suggests. "That will put us close to the date we started dating last fall."

"I don't care what the date is; as long as I'm the one you're walking toward, I'm all for it."

"You're making this too easy." She lights up, kissing me again.

"No, Linds. You're the one who's made it easy. Easy to love you, easy to want you in my life. The way you treat my daughter like she's your own is something that I can never thank you enough for. I know that I never have to worry about choosing one of you over the other. You complete me."

"I guess it's a good thing we gave in to that rumor going 'round about us last fall, then." She laughs, and I can't help it; I place her on the bed and make love to my fiancée, not stopping until we're both satisfied and exhausted.

EPILOGUE
LINDSAY

Three years later

I ROLL OVER IN BED, FEELING LIKE A WHALE AT FORTY WEEKS *—and five fucking days, not that I'm counting or anything*—it really isn't fair how often I have to get up and pee every night. I know it's for a good reason and all, but damn if this baby can't stay off my bladder for more than five minutes at a time.

"Are you okay?" Tucker asks, half asleep.

"Peachy," I snap at him, "I've only gotten up five times tonight to pee."

"Sorry, babe. Our boy's running out of room in there," he says, standing up to help me heft myself out of bed. I have the world's best husband. He's been so understanding and helpful these last few months. Dealt with every craving and pain brought on by carrying his ginormous child. I mean, don't get me wrong, I can't wait to meet our son, but I'm blaming his size on his father already.

I finally make it to the bathroom, only to pee for two seconds. "Really, body?" I call out. "All of that for two drops. Ugh." I'm so exhausted, and just need a few hours of solid sleep, and I'll feel like a new woman, but that hasn't happened in at least a week.

"Come back to bed; I'll massage your back. Is it still hurting?" Tucker asks, standing at the doorway into our bathroom. Modesty left the house about the time I moved in, which was months before we got married in the sweetest ceremony at the fire station.

"Yeah, it's spasming on and off. It's probably the start of early labor, the way the pains wrap around," I tell him as I waddle back to the bed. I lay down on my side, adjusting a pillow between my knees. Tucker aligns himself behind me, his thumbs digging right into the knots in my lower back and applying the perfect amount of pressure to help relieve some of the pain that has been bothering me. "Oh my god, that's perfect," I moan; the amount of relief I feel makes me want to cry tears of joy.

"You know they say that sex helps with bringing on labor."

"Tucker Wild, if you even think of touching me with your dick, I'll cut it off," I snap at him.

"No, you won't. You enjoy it way too much." He chuckles, calling me out on my BS.

"Okay, I might not actually cut it off your body, but I'll cut you off from sexy times."

"I think it's worth the risk. I'm going to be cut off for at least six weeks anyway, here soon," he reminds me, like I didn't know that fact.

"But, I'm finally comfortable," I whine.

"No need to change positions; just let me take care of it and make you feel good in the process. If it brings on labor, then that's just a plus. If not, well, then at least you'll feel relaxed and you might get a few hours of sleep out of the deal."

I let him take control; he shimmies my panties off my body, then lifts my leg once he's back behind me. He slips between my legs, his fingers slipping between my folds as he runs the tip of his cock along with them. His tip hits my clit and has me ready to see stars. He doesn't stall, lining his cock up with my entrance and pushing in slowly. "Holy shit," I call out as he fills me completely.

"Tell me if this is too much," he instructs, and I can't think of anything except how good it feels. Strangely enough, with him filling me, all my discomfort and pain evaporates.

"More," is the only word I can form and make come out of my mouth.

"Damn, baby, you're so tight, squeezing my cock like it's our first time," he grits out as he speeds up his thrusts from behind me. I don't know how he manages to reach around us, but his fingertips find my clit, and that's all it takes for me to fall over the edge of my orgasm. "Yes, Linds," he calls out as he thrusts through my orgasm as he chases his own. "I fucking love you," he tells me as he stills, and I can feel his body pulsing inside me as he releases.

Tucker pulls from me, heading for the bathroom for a washcloth and returning to help me clean up. Once clean, I get out of bed to pee one last time before I can, hopefully, fall back asleep. Now that it is after two in the morning, I hope to not see the clock again until around seven or eight. I waddle back to bed, sliding in and up to his side; my head finds his chest as my left leg goes over his as I attempt to wrap my body around him.

"You comfortable?" he asks a few seconds after I finally stop moving.

"Yeah," I sigh; I can feel the sleep pulling me under, finally.

"Get some sleep, baby. I love you."

"Love you," I tell him as I drift off to sleep.

"Tucker!" I yell out in a panic. "Tucker! I need you!" I yell a little louder.

"What's wrong, Linds?" he calls back, the sound of his voice getting closer as he reaches the bedroom door.

"It's time." I look at him, and I'm sure the panic is written all over my face.

"You sure?" he asks.

"Yes, I'm sure!" I snap at him. "My water broke, and I feel like I need to fucking push already." I suck in a breath and close my eyes. Our little sexcapade last night appeared to work, putting me into labor *and* getting me to sleep. So much so that I've, apparently, slept right through most of my laboring.

"Let me help you up and out to the truck. I've already got the hospital bag in the back seat, so I just need you, and we can go," he says.

"No, Tucker, it's time. Like, we're going to have this baby right here in this bed time," I tell him.

I can see the blood drain from his face as his eyes scan my body from my face to my abdomen and slightly lower.

"You sure?" he croaks out.

"I'm pretty damn sure this isn't normal labor pains." I cry out, the pain almost more than I can endure. I'd never dreamed of laboring and delivering without the aid of drugs, so lying here with nothing is not a walk in the park.

"I'm going to call an ambulance," he tells me, pulling out his phone. You'd think the man could handle a woman in labor. It isn't like he's never responded to a woman in labor call before. "Hang in there, babe; the ambulance is less than two minutes out."

"I can't wait," I pant out, my body pushing without me.

"The dispatcher wants me to check and see if I can see the baby's head," he tells me, just as a contraction finally lets up.

"Okay, help me, then," I tell him, and he sets his cell down on the end table next to the bed. I can hear the dispatcher giving him instructions on what to look for once I'm rolled onto my back.

"I can definitely see the top of the head," he tells both of us.

"Okay, have your wife take a deep breath on her next contraction and bear down; if the head comes out, have her stop pushing until you can make sure the cord isn't wrapped around the baby's neck. Hopefully, before that happens, the ambulance will be on site. They should be about thirty seconds out."

"You are doing fantastic, baby. Just a few more minutes," Tucker tells me, cheering me on as I, apparently, am going to give birth at home, completely unplanned.

"I can hear the ambulance pulling in," Tucker says, for both the dispatcher and me to hear.

"Can they get in without you going to the door?" she asks.

"Yes, tell them to come to the front door and down the hall," he tells her. It doesn't take them long to make their way inside and to my side. The paramedics take over for Tucker, which allows him to come up and help keep me as calm as possible, all while I deliver our baby in bed.

"Congratulations, it's a boy," the paramedic that delivered our son calls out. I look down and am in awe as they place him on my chest. I kiss the top of Brody's head as tears slide down my cheeks.

"You did it, babe," Tucker says into my ear. He kisses the side of my face multiple times as he looks at the two of us. "You were such a rock star."

"Do you have a towel you don't mind ruining?" one of the paramedics asks.

"Of course, let me grab one," Tucker says, stepping away and grabbing one from the bathroom. They wrap our son up in it. He's still attached to the umbilical cord, so they clamp it and hand over the special scissors to Tucker, offering for him to cut it. He does, and they help get me moved to the stretcher.

"We'll transport both mom and baby to the hospital to be checked out. If you want to follow behind us, so you have a way to get home, I'd suggest that, otherwise, you can ride in the back with us."

"I can follow," Tucker tells them; he kisses my forehead before snuggling Brody close and kissing his cheeks.

———

"EVERYTHING LOOKS GOOD," MY OB, DR. CARROLL, SAYS once she's done examining me. "How are you feeling?"

"Great, considering the events of this morning," I tell her honestly.

"I still can't believe you delivered so quickly, and at home. Remember that for next time, as they tend to come quicker, the more kids you have," she muses.

"Tucking that info away for much later. I'm not sure I'm ready to even think about that right now," I tell her. Thankfully, Brody and I checked out with flying colors. He weighed in at a whopping nine pounds nine ounces and is twenty-one inches long.

"You get some rest, the nurses will keep an eye on you, and we should be good to send you home tomorrow. If you need anything, don't hesitate to ask or have them page me," Dr. Carroll tells me, patting the end of the bed before she exits.

"Are you ready for some visitors, yet, or do you want me to keep them at bay for a little longer?" Tucker asks, sitting on the edge of my hospital bed.

"I'm ready," I tell him as I look down at our son, smiling at this amazing bundle of joy we made.

"You need to do me a favor, and sometime soon," I tell him before our room is flooded with friends and family.

"What's that, babe?" he asks.

"Go home and strip our bed before it ends up ruined from me delivering on it."

"Already taken care of. My mom went by shortly after we left and cleaned up everything. I've been told the bed is ready for you whenever you return."

"Oh, good. I worried about that the entire drive over here," I tell him just as our door opens and his parents enter, along with Paisley. She's got the biggest smile on her face and is proudly wearing a shirt that bears her "Big Sister" title. She's a pro at being a big sister, seeing as how she's got two siblings now, at her mom's house, but she's been super excited that she gets another one at our home.

"Would you like to hold your brother?" I ask her as she approaches the side of my bed, looking over the rail at him in my arms.

"Yes, please, Mom." I smile big at her. She started calling me mom shortly after Tucker and I got married, all on her own, and it was the best gift I've ever received. I made sure that Lilly was okay with it. It has never been my intention to replace her or try and step on her toes, and she realized that.

Paisley gets comfortable next to me on the bed, and I hand over her brother. I can hear the shutter clicks from someone's camera, or a phone that hasn't had the sounds turned off. I'm so grateful that someone is catching these precious moments for us.

"Tucker, get in there, and let me get your first picture

as a family of four," his mom instructs, and he flanks me on the other side. Paisley holds up Brody, and we smile for the camera. I can't wait to have that image blown up and hanging on the wall.

Today might not have gone the way I planned it, but like most of the things that have transpired over the last few years, I wouldn't change it for anything. It played out just as it was supposed to, and for that, I'm forever grateful.

———

More Lyrics & Love books are coming in 2021! Stay tuned for more information.

In the meantime, fall in love with Sam & Lauren in Marry Me!

AFTERWORD

I hope you have enjoyed this book, and would consider leaving a review on your favorite retailer.

If you would like to connect more with Samantha, please join her reader group on Facebook!

COMING SOON

Indianapolis Eagles Series Book 9
Winter 2021

Indianapolis Lightning Series Book 3
Spring 2021

ALSO BY SAMANTHA LIND

INDIANAPOLIS EAGLES SERIES

Just Say Yes ~ Scoring The Player

Playing For Keeps ~ Protecting Her Heart

Against The Boards ~ The First Intermission

The Hardest Shot ~ The Game Changer

Box Set 1 {Books 1-3}

STANDALONE TITLES

Tempting Tessa

Until You ~ An Aurora Rose Reynolds Happily Ever Alpha
Crossover Novella

Until Her Smile ~ An Aurora Rose Reynolds Happily Ever
Alpha Crossover Novella

Cocky Doc ~ A Cocky Hero Club Novel

LYRICS & LOVE SERIES

Marry Me ~ Drunk Girl

INDIANAPOLIS LIGHTNING SERIES

The Perfect Pitch ~ The Curve Ball

ACKNOWLEDGMENTS

To everyone who has supported me, thank you! Thank You for the impact you have made on my life and my writing. Please know that I appreciate you all!

xoxo,

Samantha

ABOUT THE AUTHOR

Samantha Lind is a contemporary romance author. Having spent the first 27 years of her life in Alaska, she now calls Iowa home, where she lives with her husband and two sons. She enjoys spending time with her family, traveling, reading, watching hockey (Go Knights Go!), and listening to country music.

Connect with Samantha in the following places:
www.samanthalind.com
samantha@samanthalind.com

Reader Group
Samantha Lind's Alpha Loving Ladies
Good Reads
https://goo.gl/t3R9Vm
Bookbub
https://goo.gl/4XyyLk
Newsletter
https://bit.ly/FDSLNL

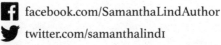

facebook.com/SamanthaLindAuthor
twitter.com/samanthalind1
instagram.com/samanthalindauthor